"The name's Dooley James, ma'am. I'm sorry for any inconvenience, but I thought I was saving your life."

Marina stared at the man before her as if he'd lost his mind. "What do you think you're doing bursting into my apartment?" she demanded.

"I was across the way and thought you were in trouble. I hope I didn't hurt you."

She sighed. "Mr. James, it's obvious you're new to this city. People here don't act like this. When they see trouble, they don't become avenging angels, and they certainly don't crawl through windows."

"Now that's a damn shame," he said in a low Southern drawl.

"Well, thank you for your efforts, Mr. James...."

"Dooley." He offered her an open, charming smile. "I figure if we're going to be neighbors, we may as well be on a first-name basis."

Dear Reader,

The holiday season is upon us and what better present to give or receive than a Silhouette Romance novel. And what a wonderful lineup we have in store for you!

Each month in 1992, we're proud to present our WRITTEN IN THE STARS series, which focuses on the hero and his astrological sign. Our December title draws the series to its heavenly conclusion when sexy Sagittarius Bruce Venables meets the woman destined to be his love in Lucy Gordon's *Heaven and Earth*.

This month also continues Stella Bagwell's HEARTLAND HOLIDAYS trilogy. Christmas bells turn to wedding bells for another Gallagher sibling. Join Nicholas and Allison as they find good reason to seek out the mistletoe.

To round out the month we have enchanting, heartwarming love stories from Carla Cassidy, Linda Varner and Moyra Tarling. And, as an extra special treat, we have a tale of passion from Helen R. Myers, with a dark, mysterious hero who will definitely take your breath away.

In the months to come, watch for Silhouette Romance stories by many more of your favorite authors, including Diana Palmer, Annette Broadrick, Elizabeth August and Marie Ferrarella.

The authors and editors at Silhouette Romance love to hear from our readers, and we'd love to hear from *you!*

Happy reading from all of us at Silhouette!

Anne Canadeo
Senior Editor

HOMESPUN HEARTS
Carla Cassidy

Silhouette
ROMANCE™
Published by Silhouette Books New York
America's Publisher of Contemporary Romance

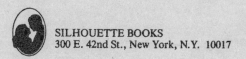

SILHOUETTE BOOKS
300 E. 42nd St., New York, N.Y. 10017

HOMESPUN HEARTS

ISBN: 0-373-08905-8

First Silhouette Books printing December 1992

Printed in the U.S.A.

CARLA CASSIDY

is the author of ten young-adult novels. She's been a cheerleader for the Kansas City Chiefs football team and has traveled the East Coast as a singer and dancer in a band, but the greatest pleasure she's had is in creating romance and happiness for readers.

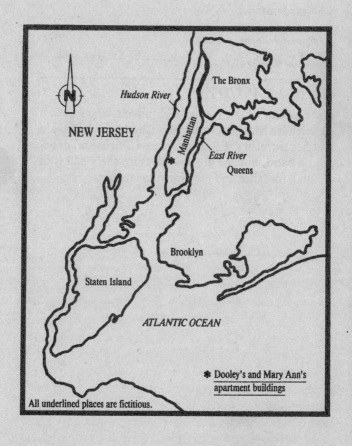

The Bronx

Hudson River

NEW JERSEY

Manhattan

East River

Queens

Brooklyn

Staten Island

ATLANTIC OCEAN

✱ Dooley's and Mary Ann's
apartment buildings

All underlined places are fictitious.

Chapter One

Dooley James stepped into the strange apartment, cursing as he fumbled for the light and bumped his shinbone against a piece of furniture in the darkness. He sighed with relief as he found the switch and the room filled with light. He dropped his suitcase to the floor and sank down into the ugly, overstuffed chair that had connected with his leg. God, what a day. He'd flown in to Kennedy Airport that morning and rented a car, then had spent the remainder of the day trying to find this address.

People on the streets of New York had to be the most frightened, paranoid people he'd ever seen in his life. Three times he'd tried to ask for directions, and each person he'd asked had looked at him as if he were an alien come to wreak havoc on their fair city. The few who had talked to him had instantly made him sorry he'd asked.

He now looked around the room with interest. His secretary knew the person who lived here, a photographer who was out of the country on assignment. She'd made all the arrangements for Dooley to stay here for the next couple of weeks, or however long it took for him to conduct his business. And if today was any indication of the friendliness of New York City, he couldn't wait to accomplish what needed to be done and get the hell back to South Carolina.

But for now the apartment was home, and he viewed his surroundings curiously. The place was small, but tidy. A daybed against one wall served as the bedroom, but Dooley didn't mind the cramped quarters. Anything was better than the impersonal air of a hotel. Besides, at least here he could cook his own meals, although he would miss his gourmet kitchen back home. He looked woefully at the ancient two-burner electric stove.

Speaking of kitchens, the first thing he had to check out was how well stocked the refrigerator was. He was starving. He pulled himself out of the chair and went over to the kitchenette, opening the refrigerator and frowning. Empty. Not a jar of mustard, not even a single piece of wilted lettuce, nothing, *nada*, zilch. Damn, his secretary had assured him that she would see that groceries were carried in before he arrived. The empty refrigerator meant he was going to have to venture out again before he could relax and call it a night. There was no way he'd be able to sleep with his stomach growling like a chain saw on a wintry morning.

He walked over to the window, surprised to find himself staring directly into the apartment in the building across the narrow alley. The buildings were so near, he could almost jump from his window right into the one across from his. How could people live in such close quarters?

He started to turn away, but paused, his attention caught by movement in the apartment across the way. A woman stepped into his line of vision. She had her back to him. She was short and dainty, and her dark hair fell in riotous curls to her well-shaped derriere. As he watched, a man also came into his view. The man was thin and short, but his face was twisted with a grimace of anger, and in his hand—a gun.

Adrenaline fired through Dooley as he realized he was watching a real-life drama unfolding before his very eyes. The man backed the woman up against the wall, and Dooley knew he had to do something, anything, to help her. He quickly assessed the situation. By the time he ran out of his building and into hers, stopping to explain the situation to the doorman who guarded the building entrance, it might be too late. The phone…he should call 911. He looked around the room frantically. Hell, he didn't even know if there was a phone, let alone where it was located in the unfamiliar apartment.

Drastic situations called for drastic measures. He swung a leg out his window and stepped out onto the platform of the old, rusted fire escape. For a moment, he gripped tightly to the railing of the iron stairs, almost dizzying in their steepness.

"Not exactly like climbing trees back home," he muttered. Racing down the steep steps, he felt the structure shake ominously beneath him.

He hit the ground running. He moved across the alley and grabbed the railing of the stairs that led upward on the outside of the building where he'd seen the life-and-death scene unfolding.

Let me get there before something horrid happens, he thought as he took the stairs two at a time, his blood making his heartbeat resound in his ears. When he reached the window, he didn't waste any time on amenities, but instead dived through toward the man with the gun, delivering a tackle that would have made a professional football coach proud.

A grunt came from the man beneath him. A scream pierced the air, and suddenly he found himself being attacked from behind by a fiery, feminine whirlwind. It took a moment for Dooley to realize that the man beneath him was not fighting, but the woman on his back had a handful of his hair and yanked at it with the ferocity of a mountain lion.

Dooley prided himself on being a man able to withstand a great amount of physical pain, but just as Sampson's weakness had been his hair, so was Dooley's. "Hey, let go of my hair," he bellowed. He twisted off the man on the floor and tried to buck her off his back, but she rode him like a professional bull-rider, her heels digging into his sides, never releasing her death-grasp on his hair.

"Who are you?" She huffed with exertion as she tightened her grip.

"I'm...would you let go?" Dooley grimaced, feeling his hair being lifted out by its roots. He looked up to see the man with the gun approaching once again. With an agile movement, Dooley reached up and slapped the gun out of his hand, then flipped her over on her back and pinned her arms above her head. "Calm down," he breathed heavily. "And don't even think about it," he said to the man, who was tiptoe-ing toward him with a heavy vase in one hand. "I don't want a hassle, I thought you were in trouble," he explained, keeping a firm grip on the woman's arms as she bucked and kicked to escape from his grasp. Finally, accepting defeat, she lay still. For a moment they lay motionless, nose to nose, their breaths warming each other's faces as they panted from their efforts.

Dooley took a moment to study the woman he'd thought he was saving. She had a cloud of dark, curly hair, eyes the color of a Carolina sky, a smattering of freckles across the bridge of a pert nose, and a mouth that was just made for kissing.

"The name's Dooley James, ma'am. I'm sorry for any inconvenience, ma'am, but I thought I was sav-ing your life."

Marina stared at the man on top of her. He wasn't handsome in the traditional sense. His curly, russet-colored hair had no definite style and looked as if a flick of a comb wouldn't hurt. A full beard and mustache just a shade darker than the hair on his head covered his lower face, but didn't quite hide the sensual curve of his full lips. His eyes were the green of the hills back home, and Marina found herself staring into them for an endless moment. Then he smiled, and his attractiveness instantly became apparent. His eyes lit with humor, and his facial expression promised a sensitivity, a depth of emotions and feelings that were infinitely appealing. She suddenly became aware of their position, the fact that he was big... he stretched twice her length on the floor, and she could feel the solid muscle of his body hovering above her.

"Ma'am, if you promise you won't pull my hair again, I'll let you up and I can explain this whole thing." His voice was low, with a Southern drawl that was at once entrancing and irritating.

"For Pete's sake, Marina, tell him you won't pull his hair. I think he's okay." Gregory Pierce had recovered the gun and now looked at Dooley with a small smile of amusement.

Marina flushed and nodded, relieved when he rolled off her and allowed her to get to her feet. She watched warily as he did the same. She was right, he was big. He stood at least six foot two. "What do you think you're doing, bursting into my apartment?" she demanded, placing her hands on her hips and facing him angrily.

"I was across the way." He gestured out the window. "I happened to glance over here and this man had a gun and I thought you were in trouble."

"This man does have a gun," Marina explained impatiently.

Gregory smiled and squirted Dooley with a burst of water. "Bang, you're dead."

"A squirt gun," she added needlessly.

"We were rehearsing a scene for an audition."

"Ah, you're actors," Dooley exclaimed, pulling a handkerchief from his well-worn jeans pocket and swiping off the water from his face.

"I'm Gregory Pierce from across the hall." Gregory held out his hand to Dooley.

"Dooley James. I just flew in to town this morning from South Carolina. I hope I didn't hurt you."

"Nah, I've had critics who hit harder," Gregory replied with a grin.

Marina straightened a lamp shade that had gotten knocked askew in the fracas. There was something about the man that irritated her. Perhaps it was his accent, so reminiscent of home and all she had tried to put behind her. "Mr. James, it's obvious you're new in this city. People in New York don't act like this. People in this city draw their shades when they see trouble—they don't become avenging angels, and they certainly don't crawl through windows."

"Now that's a damn shame," he said with an honesty that only served to make Marina dislike him even more.

"Well, thank you for your efforts, Mr. James...."

"Dooley." He offered her an open, charming smile. "I figure if we're going to be neighbors we may as well be on a first-name basis."

"Fine. Thank you, Dooley. Now, if you'll excuse us, we have work..."

"I didn't catch your name."

Marina frowned, realizing she had a headache starting right in the center of her forehead, threatening to expand out and engulf her entire body. What was this man doing in her apartment, and why did he have to have that smooth, Southern accent? "My name is Mary Ann Rayburn." Something about him caused her to lapse backward in time, and she instantly caught herself, her voice sharp as she continued. "I mean, Marina...my name is Marina Burns."

He grinned, a slow, lazy one that started at one corner of his sexy mouth, then slowly overtook his eyes. "Which is it? Mary Ann or Marina?"

Marina flushed, looking over at Gregory, who leaned against the refrigerator, watching the conversation in open amusement. "My name is Marina. It used to be Mary Ann, but I changed it."

"Why?"

"Because I wanted to," she snapped, wanting only to get him out of her apartment. "Now, if you'll excuse us, we have work to do."

"Okay, but I think you're making a big mistake."

"I beg your pardon?"

Dooley fought the impulse to reach out and push away the strand of hair that hung over her left eye. He wanted to see all of her lovely face. "Your name... Mary Ann suits you." With these words he gave her another smile, nodded at Gregory, then walked out of the apartment.

Once he had gone, Marina turned and looked at Gregory. "I don't know what you're smirking about, but I really wish you'd stop."

"I was just thinking how quickly the veneer of the big city ebbs away. As you were talking to him, I caught a hint of your hillbilly accent creeping in."

"The man is a nut case," Marina retorted, deciding to ignore Gregory's observation.

"No, you're the nut case. How many times have I told you that you should get security bars for that window? With that fire escape right outside, it's dangerous not to have them."

"I'd feel as if I was living in a jail," she returned.

"Better safe than sorry. Anyway, you were lucky it was somebody like Dooley who burst in here. He seems a rather likable man. Sort of unspoiled and untainted by the cynicism of New York." Gregory pushed himself away from the refrigerator. "Well, shall we try the scene again? And this time, try to put more fear into it. Remember," he said with a wry grin, "I'm not asking you to go shopping, I'm supposed to be threatening your life."

"Maybe I should just skip this particular audition," Marina said, sinking down onto the sofa, her eyes darkened with frustration. "I'm never going to get it right." She sighed heavily.

"Hmm, maybe you're right," Gregory agreed, sitting cross-legged in the chair next to the sofa. "And while you're at it, why don't you go back to using your real name, pack your bags, and return to that little Podunk Arkansas town where you were raised."

Marina gave her friend a scathing glare. "Don't be so melodramatic."

"Darling, I'm supposed to be melodramatic, I'm an actor."

"And a working actor at that," Marina replied with a sigh. "I've been here a whole year, and so far nothing has happened to me."

"That's not true. You've been mugged twice."

Marina grimaced. "Yes, and lost on a subway for hours, but that wasn't exactly what I meant. And don't forget the friendly exhibitionist who greets me every morning when I buy the newspaper." She swept a strand of her long, permed brown hair behind one ear. "I'm no closer to realizing my dreams than I was one year ago when I was still in Arkansas."

"Ah, New York City, she's a cold, unfeeling witch," Gregory said with a grin. He sprang up out of the chair and pulled himself to his full five foot three as he began to pace the small area in front of the sofa. "New York, she's a town without pity, a wicked tramp who devours aspiring actors and actresses for breakfast, and belches them up hopeless and shattered." His voice took on the ring of a Shakespearean actor delivering a soliloquy to a theater full of people. "New York, the city who takes dreams and dashes them to earth...." He grunted as the throw pillow she threw at him hit him square on the head. "Everyone's a critic," he said with a laugh.

"How about a cup of coffee before we rehearse any more?" Marina suggested, getting up off the sofa. She padded over to the kitchen, which was really no more than a stove, a sink and mini-refrigerator against one wall. "Damn," she muttered, opening the canister and peering into the bottom to see several lonely-looking dark grinds. "How about a cup of tea instead?"

"No, I've got some coffee. I'll be right back." Gregory disappeared out the apartment door. She leaned against the sink and smiled.

Luck had been shining down on her the day she rented this studio apartment across the hall from Gregory Pierce. In the past year he had become surrogate big brother, confidante, mentor and more often than not, the voice of sanity in what seemed at times an insane way to live.

There were days when Marina wondered if she wasn't just a little bit crazy. She had to be to keep pace with the life she'd designed for herself. She worked weekends as a waitress in a busy restaurant, and baby-sat most weeknights the two children who lived on the fifth floor. She made just enough money to pay the rent and utilities, occasionally purchase a bag of groceries, and pay for the weekly drama lessons from a woman named Holiday Maxwell. She kept her days free to attend auditions, waiting for the big break that would lift her out of her mundane existence and make her a star.

She turned toward the front door as Gregory came back in. "Here you go." He handed her a plastic container. "There should be enough there for a couple of days."

Marina smiled her gratitude. "This will hold me until payday down at the restaurant." She quickly made the coffee. While they waited for the dark brew to be ready, they sat down at the small kitchen table.

"This is new," Gregory observed, running his hand over the wooden surface of the tiny table.

Marina nodded. "I found it out by the curb on trash day. It has a broken leg." She gestured beneath the table where one wooden stub was propped on a stack of books.

"Ah, the sacrifices we make to attain our dreams," Gregory said with a rueful grin.

"Do you ever wonder if it's worth it?" Marina asked, propping her elbows up on the table and resting her chin in her hands.

"Nightly." Gregory grinned. "I've come to the startling conclusion that all actors and actresses are missing a portion of their brain. It's what makes them willing to put up with working menial jobs, paying drama coaches, subjecting themselves to the daily rejection that comes with the business." His smile widened. "The good part is that actors hang out with other actors, so they never realize they're missing an important piece of their brain."

Marina laughed. As always when she felt doubtful or insecure about the direction of her life, Gregory put her back on line, gave her the confidence and determination to continue onward. She didn't want to go back to being just plain old Mary Ann Rayburn, from Livingston, Arkansas. Since the time she was a small child, she'd wanted to be important, she wanted to matter . . . she wanted to be Marina Burns, actress extraordinaire. She got up to pour their coffee.

"Oh, I wanted to ask you something," Gregory said as he took the cup from her. "You know those little stuffed mice you make?" Marina nodded and rejoined him at the table. "My nephew's birthday is next month and I was wondering if I could buy one from you."

Marina shook her head. "No, but I'd be glad to give you one."

"I couldn't let you do that. I know the kind of time and detail work that goes into each one," he protested.

Marina smiled and placed one of her hands over Gregory's. "I'd like to give you one. Consider it a token of my appreciation. You're a good friend, Gregory. There are days I don't know what I'd do without you."

To her surprise, Gregory blushed. Their close friendship was something they enjoyed, but never discussed. "Well, darling, somebody had to be your friend. You were such a hopeless greenhorn when you first arrived here. You didn't know the first thing about surviving in the big city. If it wasn't for me, you would have turned tail and run back to Arkansas, where you would have returned to being Mary Ann Rayburn. You would have married some big old country boy like that Dooley fellow, and been pregnant and barefoot for the rest of your life."

"Not a chance," Marina protested. "Mary Ann Rayburn is dead...long live Marina Burns." She held up her coffee cup in the gesture of a toast, and Gregory touched his to hers.

"Now, let's see if Marina Burns can get this scene right for the audition tomorrow."

They worked for another hour, going over the scene another dozen times, then Marina called it quits.

"No more," she protested. "Let's call it a night. I need to do a little cleaning and want to wash my hair. Besides, if I don't know the scene by now, I'm never going to get it."

"Okay, then I'll come by for you at eight in the morning. The audition starts at nine." With this, Gregory saluted a goodbye, then disappeared out the apartment door.

When he was gone, Marina carefully locked the door, then sat back down onto the sofa, her thoughts drifting back to the man who'd burst into the apartment to save her. Dooley James...he'd been like an injection of home, causing a strange, gnawing ache in the pit of her stomach. Surely she couldn't be home-sick... impossible. How could she be homesick for a place she hated? The man had simply stirred old memories of a time and place she'd rather forget.

Imagine, playing the good Samaritan in New York. For that matter, why was Dooley James in New York? He'd said he'd just arrived from South Carolina. What was a country bumpkin like him doing here? She shoved her curiosity aside, not wanting to dwell on thoughts of the attractive country man anymore.

For the next hour, she concentrated on cleaning the small studio apartment, then pulled out the couch that made into a bed. As she worked, she focused again on the lines of the script for her morning audition.

Dooley sat in the darkness of his apartment, his earlier hunger forgotten as he thought of the woman in the apartment across the alley. Mary Ann Ray-burn... she was definitely not a native New Yorker. He'd heard the drawl that had colored her words as she'd been talking to him.

She was younger than he'd first thought, probably not much older than twenty-three, twenty-four. She was beautiful. Not the glamour of a model, but the down-home prettiness that came from within. And something about her had struck an answering chord in Dooley's heart. He'd seen her only moments, talked to her only briefly, but it had been long enough for him to realize he wanted to see her again.

He rose from his chair and went over to his window, looking into her apartment. He wasn't the type to be a Peeping Tom, but something about her drew him, pulled at him, a certain look in her eyes...one that spoke of unhappiness, loneliness.

Dooley had never been unhappy a day in his life, but he had known loneliness, the deep, abiding kind that ate at him night and day. It was an emotion he'd become intimately familiar with, especially in the past year.

He warmed as he caught sight of her. She wore some sort of an oversize T-shirt that exposed the shapeliness of her legs. She was making the couch up into a bed. The couch was near the window, which Dooley noticed was open to ease the warmth of the late spring night.

On impulse, he raised his window and leaned out. "Mary Ann," he yelled across the alley. She started, jumping in surprise at the sound of his voice, then crossed to the window, her forehead wrinkling charmingly. "I just wanted to tell you it was nice meeting you."

"Dooley James, this is not South Carolina. We are not backyard neighbors, and people in New York don't yell from window to window."

"Shut up," a gruff voice yelled from an apartment below her.

Dooley grinned. "I guess it's going to take me a while to get used to this New York stuff. Good night, Mary Ann."

"The name is Marina," she yelled back, then slammed down her window as if to punctuate the end of her sentence.

Dooley crossed over to his chair and sat back down, a smile playing on his features. Mary Ann Rayburn... what a hell of a woman.

Chapter Two

"Good morning, my little ray of sunshine," Gregory greeted Marina with a cheerful grin the next morning.

"Ugh, it should be against the law for anyone to smile before 10.00 a.m.," Marina growled, locking her apartment door and joining him in the hallway.

"Haven't you ever heard the old saying, 'the early bird catches the worm'?"

"I don't want a worm, I want an acting job," she retorted, refusing to budge from her foul mood. She'd spent a miserable night, tossing and turning with dreams of a giant, copper-haired man chasing her through the woods. She didn't know why she desperately ran to escape him, but she'd awakened exhausted and irritated that the country bumpkin across the alley had not only managed to disrupt her peace, but invade her dreams, as well.

"So, what do you have on this evening?" Marina asked, deciding to try to be pleasant. After all, it wasn't Gregory's fault that she'd had such a horrid night's sleep.

Gregory grinned at her. "I'm hoping you and I will be enjoying a sumptuous meal, celebrating our new roles in the play."

Marina returned his grin. "That would be wonderful." Her smile faded. "But I have to baby-sit tonight."

Gregory grimaced. "Ah, the children from hell."

Marina laughed at his description. "Oh, they aren't that bad. I'll admit Robert is a bit precocious, and Susan is a little curious, but basically they're good kids."

"Right, and basically Jack the Ripper was a good fellow," Gregory remarked dryly as they stepped out of the building and into the early morning sunshine. "What those kids need is some firm, male discipline. They need a father."

Marina smiled in agreement, then cast him a teasing grin. "Are you volunteering for the job?"

Gregory's face twisted in horror. "Perish the thought," he exclaimed. "I'm strictly bachelor material. Besides, Josie Wells and I would kill each other inside of ten minutes if locked in a room together."

"Josie's not that bad, she's a good woman," Marina protested in defense of their upstairs neighbor and her friend. "She does the best she can by those kids. It's difficult being a single parent. She's a good mother, and she would make somebody a wonderful wife."

"Well, not me. A wife and kids would seriously cramp my style as a promising sex symbol."

"Oh, yeah, I keep forgetting about your sex-symbol status," Marina said with a laugh, her laughter stopping abruptly as they approached the newspaper stand where she always grabbed a copy of the morning paper. This was usually the place where an elderly flasher bared his soul, but this morning, he was nowhere to be seen. Instead, standing in front of the newsstand looking handsome and cheerful, was Dooley. Marina stifled a groan. The last person she wanted to see at the moment was the man who had haunted her dreams all night long.

"Hey, good morning." Dooley spotted them and grinned widely. The smile made Marina's heart skip a beat. She'd forgotten that smiles could hold such warmth, such unabashed invitation. You rarely got those kinds of facial expressions from people on the streets of New York City.

"'Morning, Dooley," Gregory greeted the big man in an unusual burst of friendliness. "I'm glad to see you survived your first night here."

"I survived, but it will take me a while to get used to the noise."

Marina groaned inwardly. Did he plan on being here long enough to adjust? She couldn't help but notice how vivid he looked, how vibrant and alive as the morning sun played on his autumn-colored hair and beard. They were surrounded by three-piece-suit types, scurrying to catch subways, checking their watches with wrinkled brows. Dooley wore a short-sleeved denim work shirt that stretched taut across his broad shoulders. His worn, faded jeans clung to his long legs as if tailor-made. He looked like a mighty oak tree rising out of a square of concrete, completely out of place, totally unexpected.

Marina could smell him from where she stood, a curious blend of mountain pines, morning air and countryside. It was entrancing and she took a step backward as if to ward off the scent. She touched Gregory's shoulder lightly. "We'd better go. We don't want to be late."

"Oh, yeah, right." He smiled at Dooley. "We've got to run. We're on our way to a big audition."

"Good luck," Dooley said, his gaze lingering on Marina.

"Thanks," Marina answered with a flush, refusing to meet his eyes. There was something there in the green depths that called to her, beckoned her, something she didn't want to recognize, refused to acknowledge.

"Hey, why don't the two of you come to my place for dinner tonight?" he asked before they turned to walk away.

"Thanks, but I'm busy tonight," Marina replied, looking at Gregory expectantly.

"I'd love to come," Gregory said.

"Great. Let's say around six. I'm in apartment 415."

Gregory nodded and with a wave goodbye, he and Marina turned and walked toward the subway.

"Traitor," Marina muttered beneath her breath, her foul mood of earlier returning full force.

"What is your problem where Dooley James is concerned?" Gregory asked as they descended the stairs to the subway station. "He seems to be a nice enough person."

"I don't have a problem. I just don't like him," Marina snapped, feeding her token into the machine and passing through the turnstile.

"How can you not like him?" Gregory hurried to catch up with her, stopping as they came to the platform to wait for the arrival of the train. "What's not to like? He's friendly and personable, and he's just arrived and has no friends."

"That doesn't mean I have to be his friend," Marina retorted.

Gregory looked at her curiously. "I've never seen you so unreasonable. Methinks the lady doth protest too much," he said with a sly grin.

Marina glared at him. "Methinks you doth talk too much," she returned. The train thundered to a halt before them with a loud screech and the doors opened. "I don't want to talk about Dooley James anymore. I don't even want to think about him. I just want to concentrate on getting a part in this play. That's the most important thing in my life.'' With these words, Marina stomped into the train and found a seat.

Dooley watched as Marina and Gregory walked toward the subway station, his thoughts on the woman as he watched the unconscious wiggle of her derriere.

She'd looked like a Marina this morning, with her hair confined in a braid, and her freckles artfully concealed beneath skillfully applied makeup. She'd looked beautiful, but Dooley preferred the way she had looked the night before, with her hair a wild cascade of curls and her skin glowing with health, exposing each one of those exquisite freckles. Yes, she'd looked beautiful this morning, but it was as if she wore a mask of sophistication to hide the woman beneath.

Dooley pulled thoughtfully on his beard. He knew nothing about Mary Ann Rayburn, and yet when he'd looked into her dark blue eyes, he felt as if he'd known her forever. It had been strange, in a sort of crazy and wonderful way. There was a force there, a sort of magic at work. He grinned wryly at his own fanciful thoughts.

He paid for his newspaper, then walked back to his apartment. As he went, he smiled greetings to the people he passed, their reactions amusing to him. Some of the people merely ignored him, others cautiously returned his good-morning, a few looked at him as if he'd lost every one of his marbles. Back home in South Carolina you couldn't walk ten feet down any street without three people stopping you to ask about your family, your health or your business.

Yes, New York City was a strange sort of place, but it was the logical choice for his sixth Country Cookin' Restaurant. With each restaurant he'd opened, he'd tried bigger and bigger cities. When the ones in Chicago and Kansas City had done so well, he ached to go all out and tackle the Big Apple.

It was still hard for him to comprehend that the skills he'd learned while cooking meals for his brothers and sisters when growing up had transformed into a business that made Dooley, at the age of thirty, one of the most successful restaurateurs in the whole United States.

Dooley should be excited about establishing another in his chain of restaurants, but he simply couldn't summon up any enthusiasm. Lately he'd felt a sort of restlessness in his soul, a sort of longing for some indefinable something that refused to be named. He'd hoped the challenge of making one of his restaurants work in New York City would soothe the restlessness, but so far it hadn't helped.

Dooley shook his head as he entered his apartment. He'd been out earlier that morning and had fully stocked both the refrigerator and the canned goods. He looked at his wristwatch, noting that it would still be a couple of hours before he heard from the real-estate agent who was handling the task of finding Dooley a perfect restaurant site. There was plenty of time for him to cook himself a good old-fashioned breakfast.

As always, when cooking Dooley was at peace. For as long as he could remember, he'd loved to cook. There was something pleasing in the art of creating good food.

Dooley had learned long ago that people dined out for a variety of reasons, and not always simply because they were hungry. In his restaurants he'd gone out of his way to create an atmosphere that not only fed taste buds, but the soul, as well. Country Cookin' Restaurants boasted not only excellent country cuisine, but a relaxed atmosphere that surrounded the customers, comforted them and invited them to linger. Smiling at thoughts of his business, he crumbled freshly ground sausage into a frying pan.

Following breakfast, he received a call from the real-estate agent, who gave him a list of locations he deemed appropriate for Dooley's restaurant. Dooley decided to venture out and look over the general areas the agent had mentioned. Besides, he wanted to get a look at the city that had inspired songs and books.

He opted to hail a cab, forgoing the uncertainty of trying to learn the subway systems. He'd heard horror stories about that particular form of transportation. Besides, the thought of traveling underground at breakneck speeds made a funny panic press at his chest.

However, Dooley quickly discovered that getting a cab for himself was a study in futility. He hailed two, watching other people claim each of them before he could get to them.

Finally, barreling to the edge of the curb, he stopped a cab and yanked open the back door. "Whew, I thought I was going to stand on that corner all day. I kept losing taxis to other people."

"Aggression. That's what it takes to survive in this city," the driver said, talking around a smoldering butt of a cigar clenched tightly between his teeth. "Where to, Mac?"

"The name's Dooley," he said as he slid into the back seat, "and I'm not sure," he added thoughtfully. "Let's just drive around a little bit."

The driver stared at him in the rearview mirror. "Just drive?"

Dooley smiled. "I want to get a feel for the city. This is my first trip to New York."

"Gosh, I'd a never guessed it," the driver exclaimed, pulling away from the curb amid honking horns.

Dooley decided to ignore the driver's sarcasm and instead focused on the scenery around him.

He began to understand the magic of New York, the sense of anticipation that permeated the air, the expectancy of a happening at any moment. The streets were filled with all kinds of people from different nationalities and backgrounds. This was a city that accepted all and created its own magic through the colorful, sometimes eccentric, always fascinating people who lived and worked here.

Still, the more he understood of New York, the more he knew he could never survive here. Dooley gathered his strength from the open spaces of home. He found his peace in the green fields, the pine and hemlock forest-covered mountains, and the slower pace of South Carolina.

He was suddenly anxious to find the site for his restaurant and get back home. He could direct much of the business end from there, with bimonthly trips back here to New York.

Yes, New York was a great place to visit, but he was ready to get back home where he belonged.

Marina was silent as she and Gregory walked back toward the subway train that would take them home. Discouragement weighed heavily on her shoulders, making her feet drag. It had been a long day. She hadn't made it through the first round of the auditions, but Gregory had remained tied up all afternoon. She'd sat and waited for him, hoping that at least one of them would come away from the audition with a job. But when Gregory finally came out, his face had told the depressing story. He hadn't gotten a part, either.

"Come on kid, don't look so down. There will be other parts, other plays." He finally spoke, breaking the heavy silence between them as they took their seats on the train.

"I know." Marina sighed. "I just want this so bad."

"You and about a thousand others," Gregory observed.

"You'd think that after a year of going to audition after audition, the odds would be that one time I'd be the right type, have the right look for a part."

"It will happen to you, hon," Gregory said, putting an arm around her shoulders and giving her a squeeze. "You just have to be patient, and keep at it. I swear, I think half the secret in this business is persistence and determination."

"Well, I have plenty of that," Marina said, raising her chin in a show of strength. Nothing was going to stop her from achieving her goals, nothing was going to keep her from attaining her dreams.

"Why don't you come with me to eat at Dooley's," Gregory said as they got off the train and headed for their apartment building.

Marina shook her head. "I told you I've got to baby-sit tonight. Besides, even if I weren't busy, I wouldn't come." Her eyes darkened. "I had my fill of men like Dooley James when I was back home in Arkansas. I don't want anything to do with some good old boy who has dirt beneath his fingernails and a head full of useless dreams."

"Whew," Gregory whistled. "Somebody must have hurt you badly in that little town where you grew up."

"Don't be silly," Marina scoffed. "Nobody hurt me. I just know what I want, and getting involved with Dooley James is not how to get it. In fact, I don't want to get involved with any man. I don't have time. I have my career to consider."

"For God's sake, Marina. We're talking about a meal here, not a lifetime commitment," Gregory protested.

Marina's answer was silence. She couldn't explain to Gregory the fact that something about Dooley threatened her. Something in his eyes, the warmth of his smile, made her thinking get fuzzy, her dreams seem less important. And her desire to become an actress was the most important thing in her life. Dooley was a threat that she didn't want to explore.

Later that evening, as she waited for the water to boil for her dinner of boxed macaroni and cheese, she wondered if she hadn't made a mistake about the dinner invitation.

Through her window, along with the early-evening breeze, came the scents of something wonderful cooking across the alley. It was the smell of home cooking, the yeasty warmth of bread, the richness of fresh vegetables, the mouth-watering odor of chicken being fried. Marina's stomach rolled and grumbled in protest as she drained the pasta in the sink and added the foil package of powdered cheese flavoring, butter and the last of her milk.

She fixed herself a dish, but before sitting down at her table, she walked across the room and slammed down the window. It was bad enough that the hayseed was living right across the alley, but couldn't he at least keep his cooking smells to himself?

She had just finished eating when there was a knock on her door. It was Josie and the kids.

The buxom blonde breezed in, herding eight-year-old Robert and six-year-old Susan before her. "Hi, doll, as usual I'm late. The kids have been fed and watered and I should be home around midnight." Josie paused for breath, then continued. "I've threatened them with bodily harm if they give you any trouble."

"You know they never give me any trouble," Marina protested.

Josie paused a moment, then grinned. "Yeah, isn't it bizarre, you're the only one I know who can handle them. Well, gotta go." With this, she breezed out, leaving the kids to look at Marina expectantly.

"Are you gonna tell us mouse stories tonight?" Susan asked, pushing a strand of pale blond hair out of her eyes.

"Maybe before bedtime," Marina answered. "I thought maybe you'd like to draw pictures for a little while."

"Drawing is dumb," Robert proclaimed.

"Yeah, dumb," Susan echoed.

"Why don't you have a TV? It's dumb not to have a TV, and it's dumb to have the window closed." Robert opened the window she had shut earlier, then flopped down onto the sofa with a look of petulance on his face.

"Yeah, dumb." Susan sat down onto the sofa next to her big brother.

Marina joined them. "It sounds to me like some-body got up on the 'dumb' side of the bed this morn-ing."

Susan's little forehead crinkled into a frown. "Where's the dumb side of the bed?"

"Well, some people get up on the right side of the bed, some get up on the wrong side of the bed. Then there are the ones who get up on the dumb side," Marina improvised. "Those people get up with their heads on the floor and their feet in the air. They wear their slippers on their nose and eat breakfast with their toes."

Susan giggled. "What else?" she asked and Marina knew she was hooked.

She continued her story and within minutes, both kids were giggling at the ridiculous scenario she painted.

As she spun whimsical stories for the kids, she forgot all about the frustration of her day, the annoying presence of the man across the alley. She simply gave herself to the pure pleasure of evoking laughter from the children with her homespun tales.

The evening passed quickly and soon it was time for the kids to go to bed. Marina made up the sofa bed and tucked them in, then sat on the edge of the bed telling them stories until their eyelids drooped and their breathing slowed to the rhythm of sleep.

Settling into the chair next to where they slept, Marina picked up a basket of sewing and grabbed the mouse she'd begun working on for Gregory's nephew.

Strange, how she'd managed to turn something that had frightened her as a child into a hobby.

When she'd been little, her favorite place to play had been the old, abandoned barn that sat near her aunt and uncle's farmhouse. It had been her special place, a magical place where she could pretend to be anything she wanted to be. The first time she'd seen a mouse scurry across the floor, she'd screamed and ran, not to return to the barn for days. But eventually she had returned, and as the days passed, she'd discovered that a whole family of mice lived within the walls of the old barn. And she also realized that the mice had different features and characteristics, and many of them reminded her of people in the small town of Livingston. It wasn't long after that she began making stuffed mice with human characteristics. Much of the money that had brought her to New York had been earned by selling the delightful little creatures to the people in the small town.

She looked down, startled to see that she had been cutting red yarn for the hair of the mouse she worked on. Red...for God's sake, where had that come from? But, of course, she knew. She looked over to the window across the alley, but the apartment was in darkness. Apparently Dooley James was either already in bed, or had gone out.

Dooley was neither. He sat in the darkness on the fire-escape platform outside his window, thinking...wondering about the woman across the alley.

He'd enjoyed Gregory's company over supper, had relished the opportunity to grill the little man about Mary Ann. What he'd discovered about her only served to whet his appetite to know more. Gregory had told him she wasn't involved with anyone, that she rarely dated and that her number-one priority was her acting career. Gregory painted a picture of a woman driven to succeed, possessed by the need to be somebody.

After Gregory had left, Dooley had gone over to the window and looked out. She was there, sitting on the edge of the sofa where two children were tucked beneath white sheets. She was telling stories to the kids, and although he was too far away to be able to discern the words, he could hear the low murmur of her voice, the responding laughter of the kids. The picture made a funny catch in his heart, a vague wistfulness in his belly. He suddenly realized he was in no hurry to finish up his business and get the hell out of this city... no hurry at all.

Chapter Three

"He does something different with his pota-toes...adds a spice that I can't quite identify. The flavor is absolutely out of this world."

Marina glared at Gregory, who sat at her kitchen table sharing the last of the coffee she'd borrowed from him. She was busy ironing her waitress uniform for work that night. "Honestly, Gregory, must you drone on and on about Dooley's culinary skills? You've already told me how crisp and juicy the chicken was, how rich and creamy the gravy. The way you're talking, you'd think Dooley James was the Southern answer to Julia Child." It was bad enough that she'd smelled the meal all night. She didn't want a running commentary on it first thing this morning.

"He's not exactly a world-famous chef, but he is a professional cook," Gregory replied.

"What do you mean?" This caught her attention. The thought of Dooley puttering about in a kitchen was ludicrous. Dooley looked more like a lumberjack, or a farmer. He definitely didn't look like a man who would be at home amid pots and pans.

"He owns a successful chain of restaurants. At least that's something you two have in common."

"What?" She looked at Gregory blankly.

"Well, Dooley owns restaurants and you work in one."

Marina heaved an exasperated sigh. "That's like saying the people who clean the rest rooms at the airport have a lot in common with the pilots." She flipped the skimpy uniform over on the ironing board. "So, what's he doing in New York?"

"He wants to open one of his restaurants here."

"Oh, as if New York City doesn't have a dozen eating establishments in each block floundering on the brink of bankruptcy," she snorted. "I knew that man was crazy the minute he broke in here the other night. This only confirms it."

Gregory shrugged. "I don't know. Beneath that easygoing charm, Dooley strikes me as the kind of man who goes after what he wants and gets it. There's a lot of focused energy in him. He'd probably make a great actor."

Marina laughed at this. "Terrific, just what we need. More competition."

"He comes from a big family. He's got three younger brothers and two sisters. They seem to be real close."

"I swear, Gregory, since you met Dooley that's all you talk about. Has the man bewitched you or what?"

Gregory paused to take a sip of his coffee, then answered, "It's just been a long time since I've met somebody I like, somebody I think I could truly learn to admire."

At that moment their conversation was interrupted by a ruckus out in the hallway and a brisk knock on the door.

Marina opened it to find Josie, looking harassed and angry. "Can you watch Susan for a few minutes? Robert is up on the roof throwing water balloons on the pedestrians below."

"The kid makes Dennis the Menace look like an angel," Gregory scoffed, getting up from the table. "He needs a firm hand . . . right on his butt."

"Oh, how typically male," Josie returned. "Resort to brutality to solve a problem."

"I suppose you are going to sweet-talk the little devil down from the roof," Gregory shot back.

Together the two left Marina's apartment, arguing all the way up the stairs. Even when they disappeared from sight, their voices still rang down the stairwell. Marina smiled to herself as they left. She knew both Gregory and Josie fed on these arguments, were stimulated by their verbal antagonism toward each other. She had a feeling that beneath their enmity was a growing attraction toward each other. She'd like to see the two of them become a couple. Both of them deserved to have somebody love them.

Susan perched on the edge of the sofa and looked at Marina with a deep sigh. "Boy, Robert's going to catch it this time."

"Robert will be fine," Marina assured the little girl. She hung the freshly pressed uniform on a hanger, turned off the iron, then joined Susan on the sofa.

"So, what have you been doing this morning?" Marina asked, trying to take the little girl's mind off her brother's misbehavior and her mother's ire.

"Nothing much. Me and Robert watched cartoons. We always watch cartoons while Mommy sleeps. She doesn't want us to do anything else." They both jumped as there was a knock on the door.

"That's probably your mom," Marina said, getting up to answer it. "Oh..." she exclaimed in surprise as she opened the door and looked into Dooley's leaf green eyes. As always she was struck immediately by his attractive vitality. The man positively oozed the aura of fresh air, sunshine and good health.

"Good morning," he said, his mustache dancing as a smile curved his lips. "I whipped these up this morning and thought you might enjoy a couple." He held out a plate upon which were three of the largest, most luscious-looking cinnamon rolls Marina had ever seen. Her stomach immediately gurgled in response. She squashed her impulse to take the plate from him.

"Thank you, Dooley, but I'm dieting," she said, hoping her nose didn't grow with the blatant lie.

She didn't want to accept anything from him. Had it been Gregory who had offered them, she would have accepted without a second thought. Gregory's eyes weren't that provocative shade of green. Gregory's lips didn't hint at passion-filled kisses and secrets untold.

"A diet?" Dooley grinned at her. "Why, you're nothing but a little bit right now."

"But I'm not on a diet," Susan quipped, coming to stand next to them, her bright blue eyes widening at the sight of the rolls.

"Well, now, who do we have here?" Dooley set the plate on the table and crouched down on one knee so he was almost at eye level with the little girl. "What's your name?"

"Susan Elizabeth Wells," Susan replied, her fascination torn between the sweets on the plate, and Dooley's beard. "Is that real?" she asked, pointing to the burst of red on Dooley's chin.

"Sure, it's real. Why would you think it wasn't?"

"Robert has a beard like that, only it hooks behind his ears with wires. He wore it last Halloween and looked really silly."

"Who's Robert?" Dooley asked.

"My brother. He's up on the roof."

Dooley stood up and looked at Marina. "Up on the roof?"

Marina nodded. "Robert's mother and Gregory went up to get him down. It seems Robert thought it would be fun to go up there and pelt people down on the sidewalk with water balloons. Here they come now," she finished, hearing their voices preceding them down the stairwell.

Gregory appeared first, with Robert firmly in his grasp, and Josie brought up the rear.

"Hey, Dooley," Gregory greeted the big man with a tight smile. "You, young man, march yourself straight upstairs to your apartment. Your mother will be right there to deal with you," he said to the young boy. Robert gave Gregory a scathing glare, then stuck out his tongue and ran up the stairs to his apartment.

"I don't know what to do with him," Josie said worriedly, then smiled apologetically at Dooley. "Hi, I'm Josie Wells."

"Dooley James," Dooley replied with a nod. "He looks like a bright little boy."

"Too bright," Gregory remarked. "Much too bright to spend his time cooped up in an apartment all day. The boy needs creative stimulus."

"I tried to buy some at the store the other day, but they were fresh out," Josie said with a sarcastic look at Gregory. "Why is it that people who aren't parents always have all the answers?" With a shrug and a wave, she headed down the hallway.

"And why is it that mothers always think they know everything?" Gregory asked, following on her heels.

"Susan, come on," Josie yelled as she disappeared up the stairs.

"I guess I'd better go," Susan said, casting one last longing look at the cinnamon rolls.

Dooley grinned down at her. "You know, I'll bet nobody would mind if you took one of those home with you. In fact, you'd better take two, one for your brother."

Susan looked at Marina for affirmation. Marina nodded and with a happy grin, Susan grabbed a fat roll in each hand, then ran out into the hallway and disappeared up the steps.

"That was nice," Marina said grudgingly to Dooley.

He grinned at her. "You said you were on a diet. Besides, she's a cute kid."

Marina nodded. "They're both basically good kids. Gregory's right, the only real problem is that Robert is a typical boy, full of energy, but it's difficult to keep him occupied in a New York City apartment."

"Don't they have parks in this city? Someplace where the kids could go to use up some of that energy?"

"Sure, but Josie doesn't have time to take the kids. She's working two jobs to keep things together, and you don't dare let the kids go by themselves." She shrugged. "It's just one of those problems endemic to city living and single-parenting." She offered him a hesitant smile. "Well, thank you for the rolls."

"Actually, I had an ulterior motive for bringing them," he said, smiling at her in a way that made her realize they were completely alone. There was something about his smile that seemed to suck the oxygen out of the air, making it difficult for her to catch her breath. "I wanted an excuse to come over here so I could ask you if you'd have dinner with me this evening."

"I can't. I'm working tonight," Marina said, for the first time since she'd started the waitressing job grateful to have that as an excuse.

"Perhaps another time," he offered, and Marina nodded with what she hoped was noncommitment. "Okay, then I'll see you later," he said, reaching out and touching the tip of her nose with one finger, then turning and walking away.

She closed her apartment door and leaned against it thoughtfully, reaching up and rubbing the spot where his finger had grazed. It had been a casual, simple touch, but her nose burned as if she'd been out in the sun too long.

What was it about that man that bothered her in a way that was not altogether unpleasant? She'd been in New York City for a year, been approached by dozens of attractive, available men, but never had she felt even a hint of this unease that Dooley evoked in her by his mere presence.

She shoved herself away from the door, irritated by the fact that something about Dooley made her feel vague stirrings of desire for something...what it was, she couldn't quite put her finger on, but it was definitely a feeling she didn't want to address.

She knew better than anyone that the only way she was going to achieve her goal of becoming a famous actress was to remain focused, completely committed to her ultimate destination. There was no time for a man in her life, no place for any distractions or involvements. Besides, if and when she decided she was ready for a personal relationship, she would choose somebody who was as interested in the theater as she. She would choose someone who had the same burning desire as she did, somebody who would support her career.

She eyed the last, lonely cinnamon roll sitting on the plate on the table. No, she didn't want Dooley James in her life, but it couldn't hurt if she took one small bite of that roll.

She bit into it and closed her eyes, releasing a sigh of satisfaction at the sweet burst of cinnamon and spice. There might be something about Dooley James that got under her skin, but she had to admit he was one heck of a good cook.

"It looks like you've got a live bunch at table two," Cynthia Johnson exclaimed, joining Marina at the bar where Marina waited for the bartender to fill her order.

Marina looked over at the table where three young men were sitting, their faces flushed from alcohol and their voices a modicum too loud for the elegant atmosphere of the Red Herring Restaurant.

"They're on the verge of crossing the line from being amusingly loose to rudely obnoxious," Marina replied, smiling at the bartender as he placed the last of her order on her tray. "I hope you made this gin and tonic heavy on the tonic. I think this particular customer has had more than enough gin."

The bartender nodded. "It's light."

"Maybe they'll be drunk enough to leave you a decent tip," Cynthia offered sympathetically.

"I can only hope," Marina said, grinning at her fellow waitress, then heading for the table. "Here we are," she said, placing their refills before them and removing the empty glasses. "Is there anything else I can get you?"

"Sure, sweetheart, you can get me your phone number," the ruddy-faced blonde said, grabbing hold of her wrist before she could move away.

"I don't think your wife would approve of that," Marina answered, seeing the ring on the man's hand. She tried to pull her wrist out of his grasp, but he held tight.

"She wouldn't care. She doesn't understand me. Come on, baby, give me your phone number. I could show you a real good time."

It was obvious the man was more drunk than Marina had first thought, more drunk than the other two men at the table, who looked more embarrassed than anything.

"Hey, Joey, knock it off," one of them muttered softly, wincing as the drunk barked a loud laugh.

"Sir, you have to let go of my arm," Marina said, trying to control her growing irritation and remain pleasant.

"But I like your arm. It's a nice arm," he replied, tightening his grip.

"Sir, please let go."

"What time do you get off work? We could paint this town red," he said with a slight slur.

Marina jumped as a huge hand came out of no-where and fastened on to the drunk's. "I believe the lady asked you to kindly let go of her."

Marina looked up to see Dooley standing next to her. His voice was smooth, emanating Southern charm, but the green of his eyes was that of turbulent seas as he looked at the tipsy customer, and his jaw worked overtime to communicate something other than friendliness.

For a moment the two men played a game of non-violent war, using their eyes as weapons. Dooley was the victor as the customer released Marina's arm with a small laugh. "Hey, man, it was a joke."

"In very poor taste," Dooley observed, then turned to Marina. "Are you all right?"

"Of course," she flushed, seeing the restaurant manager approaching them.

"Is everything all right here?" he asked.

"Fine," Marina assured him. She lowered her voice and gestured to the drunken patron. "It seems he's had a little too much to drink."

"Any problems, you let me know. I'll see to it that the gentleman is escorted out."

Marina nodded, then turned to Dooley. "Thanks for your help," she said as the manager drifted back to his position at the front door of the establishment.

"Could you show me where to sit if I want to eat?" Dooley asked.

"Uh...sure..." Marina led him over to one of her empty tables, disoriented first by his presence here, but most of all by his physical appearance. He looked different. His beard had been trimmed close to his chin and instead of his uniform of jeans and work shirt, he wore a camel-colored sports coat and slacks, with a lighter beige dress shirt. Dooley in a T-shirt and a pair of jeans was handsome, but in dress clothes, he was something else again.

"What are you doing here?" she asked as he sat down.

He grinned, the slow sexy grin that made Marina's heart pump in spastic rhythm. "I figured if Mohammed wouldn't come to the mountain..."

"How did you know where I work?"

"Gregory was very helpful in informing me." Dooley leaned back in his chair and looked around. "Nice place," he commented. "Although a bit too stuffy for my taste."

She nodded, noticing the way the candlelight turned his burnished hair to flames. Even the hair on his chest, peeking out of the shirt's open neckline, sparked like embers glowing in a dying fire. She wondered if she reached out and touched his chest if it would be warm, telling her of the fires within. She handed him a menu, irritated by her fanciful thoughts. "I'll give you a few minutes to decide, then I'll be back to take your order."

"That won't be necessary," he said, handing the menu back to her. As he did, their fingers touched, a gentle brush of flesh that made her breath catch in her throat. "Just bring me whatever is the house specialty," he said, and something in his eyes told her he had been intensely aware of the casual touch of their fingers, as well.

She nodded and escaped from the table, heading toward the kitchen to turn in his order.

Dooley watched her hurrying away, his eyes lingering on the provocative sway of her shapely hips. He'd seen the surprise on her face when their hands had brushed, he'd been surprised himself by the emotions that had swept over him at their brief contact. He couldn't remember the last time desire had swept through him so quickly, so unexpectedly.

Dooley had never understood matters of the heart. He'd spent most of his adult years putting his energies into his restaurants. Now, suddenly, he realized how he'd let his personal life flounder. Strange, that it had taken a trip to New York and a woman named Mary Ann Rayburn to remind Dooley that he was not only a restaurateur, but also a man.

He watched as she scurried around the restaurant, taking orders and doing her job. He studied her critically, trying to discern exactly what it was about her that so attracted him.

She was extremely pretty. Her dark hair was pulled up in a ponytail that bobbed and jumped with every step she took. The skimpy uniform displayed her petite, but exquisitely proportioned shape to perfection. Yes, she was damned pretty, but there were lots of pretty women in South Carolina. No, it wasn't just her physical appearance that appealed to him.

Dooley was not a violent man, but when he'd walked in and saw her arm caught by the drunk, her eyes flashing not only annoyance, but also a touch of fear, he'd wanted to punch the man in his leering face. That surge of protectiveness was new and unexpected.

He smiled expectantly as she approached him carrying a salad and a basket of bread sticks. "I thought you might like the watercress salad. The dressing is one of the chef's specialties," she said, setting the salad and bread sticks down before him, then leaving the table as if the hounds of hell were chasing her.

Good, she wasn't unaffected by him. Apparently she was feeling something snapping in the air between them, as well. One thing was certain, Dooley wasn't going back to South Carolina until he'd had an opportunity to explore these alien, exciting feelings concerning Ms. Mary Ann Rayburn.

Marina tried to contain her irritation as she served the people at the table next to where Dooley sat. She was intensely aware of his eyes on her, his gaze following her every move. She could feel his interest, as potent as a touch, and she knew that eventually she was going to have to give her "my career is my life" speech.

"Who's the guy at table four?" Cynthia asked the next time she and Marina met at the bar. "He's a major hunk, and if I'm reading the signals right, he wants you for dessert."

"If that's the case, I'm going to have to redirect his signals," Marina exclaimed.

"Oh, honestly, Marina. Nobody said you couldn't have fun while you pursue your dreams," Cynthia said impatiently.

Marina shook her head. "I'm not about to dilute my ambition by having to deal with getting involved with somebody."

"I don't know, Marina." Cynthia gave her a look of amazement. "If you turn your back on a guy like that, then I think you're more fool than anything."

Marina merely shrugged as the other girl moved away. Cynthia would never understand about the burning ambition that drove Marina. Cynthia wanted to be an actress as well, but Marina had a feeling Cynthia would be just as satisfied remaining a waitress until some Prince Charming walked into her life and swept her off her feet.

Marina's ambition was stronger than that, it had been nurtured from youth. It had been the force that had sustained her through the loneliness, the emptiness. She wanted the approval of the audience, the adulation of a crowd, and nothing was going to get in her way. Nothing was going to distract her.

"Can I get you anything else?" she asked Dooley moments later. His plate was empty, attesting to the fact that he'd enjoyed the house specialty of veal cordon bleu.

"No, nothing more to eat," he declined. "But I would like to have a word with your chef. The salad dressing could use just a little bit of lemon juice and I wanted to talk to him about his potatoes. I have an idea on how to enhance the flavor."

Marina stared at him in horror. "Oh, no, Dooley, you can't tell that to Chef Reviere." Marina thought of the little Frenchman, who was known not only for his culinary skills, but for his temper tantrums, as well. "Dooley, this isn't some little country restaurant down South. Chef Reviere is a professional and doesn't take kindly to criticism."

"I don't intend to criticize," Dooley objected. "I just thought I'd pass along some little tips I've learned through the years."

"Well, it's just not done," Marina said firmly, tearing his ticket off her pad and placing it on the table. "Oh, I've got to go," she said as the people at the next table motioned for her attention.

For the next few minutes she had little time for thoughts of Dooley as she took care of her customers' needs. She was grateful when the tipsy man who'd given her a hard time left, leaving behind a more then generous tip as if to apologize for his obnoxiousness. Although the hours were good and the tips unusually healthy, one of the drawbacks of waitressing was dealing with rude or obnoxious people.

By the time she had taken care of her other customers, she noticed Dooley had left his table, but his tab still lay on the tabletop. She looked around the restaurant. Where was he?

Surely he hadn't gone back to the kitchen? This thought struck horror in her heart. Oh, that would be a catastrophe. The last time somebody had gone to talk to Chef Reviere, the little Frenchman had spent the next two hours throwing pots and pans around the kitchen, threatening to quit and return to his native France. It had taken Mr. Harlin, the owner of the restaurant, talking himself blue in the face, and the promise of a healthy raise to get the chef to settle down. Mr. Harlin had given strict orders that nobody was ever to get into the kitchen to talk to the chef again.

Marina hurried to the back of the restaurant, visualizing her termination slip being handed to her. Jobs were so hard to come by, and this was the best-tipping one she'd had since coming to New York. She'd never forgive Dooley if he managed to get her fired, and she'd never forgive Gregory for telling the big country man where she worked. What had Gregory been thinking of, anyway?

She could hear their voices before she went through the swinging saloon doors that led to the kitchen. Chef Reviere's high-pitched voice rattled in his foreign tongue.

"Frenchy, I can't understand you when you start that kind of talk," Dooley was saying when Marina swung through the doors. Marina felt her heart drop into her sensible shoes.

"But, I have never heard of this...this spice is used on meats, for Cajun flavor, not on potatoes," Chef Reviere protested, looking at Dooley in amazement. He clapped Dooley on his broad shoulders. "I must try one of these restaurants of yours someday." The little man grinned broadly.

Marina slowly backed out of the kitchen in surprise, stunned by the scene she had just witnessed. What magic was it that Dooley James possessed? What was it about him that made people on the streets of New York return his smiles, had jaded actors dining with him, and temperamental chefs clapping him on the back? What was it about him that frightened her so badly, yet at the same time pulled at her, compelled her, enticed her? She didn't know; the only thing she did know for sure was that she desperately hoped Dooley would return to South Carolina, and soon.

Chapter Four

Marina stripped off her waitress uniform in the ladies' rest room and quickly changed into a pair of jeans and a pullover sleeveless blouse.

The restaurant had closed fifteen minutes before and she was anxious to get home. Her feet were killing her and she was completely exhausted.

It had been an unusually busy night, and a strange one, thanks to Dooley. The man had remained at the restaurant for most of the night, happily ensconced in the kitchen with Chef Reviere. It had been an odd sight, the copper-haired, bearded Southerner and the diminutive, intense Frenchman, each sporting an apron and managing to surpass the language barrier. Every time Marina had sneaked a peek into the kitchen, the two had been laughing and exchanging secrets like school chums.

At least it was a good night for tips, she thought as she hung her uniform in the small utility closet, then left the rest room.

She'd made enough tonight to ease the financial crunch of late. It would get her by until the next payday. She could even repay Gregory the coffee she'd borrowed.

"Good night, doll," Nick Marcini, the manager, yelled as she headed for the front door.

"'Night Nick," she returned with a tired wave, then stepped out into the hot night air.

Marina always dreaded the walk home from work. Two o'clock in the morning was not an ideal time to stroll the city streets. But a taxi seemed a silly expense for the three-block distance and the subway was more trouble than it was worth.

Straightening her back stiffly, she headed for home. One thing she had learned was to walk tall and purposefully, acutely aware of her surroundings. It was usually people with victims' body language who actually became victims.

She had only gone a few feet when she heard heavy footsteps behind her. As a hand touched her shoulder, she whirled around, ready to use her purse as a weapon. The breath whooshed out of her in a gush. "Jeez Louise, Dooley. You scared the life out of me."

The big man smiled apologetically. "Sorry. I didn't mean to frighten you."

Marina stared up at him, noticing that he had a trace of what looked like flour on the side of his neck, and a small piece of lettuce decorated his russet hair. Still, this certainly didn't detract from his overall attractiveness . . . an attractiveness she found distinctly annoying. "What are you doing here?" she asked, her tone sharper than she intended.

"After I left the restaurant I realized I was too keyed up to go right home. Then I started thinking about you walking alone after work and I decided I didn't like the idea of you by yourself on the streets this late."

Marina stifled a groan. "Dooley, I'm a big girl, accustomed to taking care of myself."

"You're too pretty to walk home alone at this hour of the night," he replied gruffly.

Marina started to protest, wanting to exert her independence, but she was too tired to argue. Besides, there was a part of her that was perversely pleased by the fact that he found her pretty.

The last thing she wanted was to get involved with Dooley, but surely his walking her home didn't constitute a lifetime commitment, she reasoned.

"I almost missed you," he explained. "I was looking for you in your uniform."

"I never wear it out in public," Marina said. "It would be just asking for trouble to wear that skimpy thing out on the streets."

"Especially the way it looks on you," he added with open admiration.

She started walking, acutely grateful for the darkness that surrounded them. She wouldn't want him to see the warm blush she knew she wore.

"This is a strange town," he observed after a moment or two. "Back home the streets fold up by ten o'clock. But this place never sleeps." There was a touch of awe in his voice.

Marina nodded. She could relate to the way he felt. She'd experienced the same feelings when she'd first arrived here. New York City was like a strange foreign country where there were few rules and seemingly no taboos. *And it's where I belong,* she reminded herself firmly.

"Back home at this time of night, the only thing you'd be able to hear would be the wind rustling in the treetops and the insects all talking to each other." His voice was low, and as soothing as a back rub on tight muscles. "I've got a pond out back, and about this time every night there's an old bullfrog who talks to the moon. You can hear his low-throated complaints for miles."

His words brought a smile to Marina's lips. Yes, she could remember nights like that, when the darkness belonged to nocturnal creatures and the forces of nature, and a screaming siren, the whoosh of bus brakes, the honk of a taxi had no place. Her smile slowly fell. She could also remember how lonely those night sounds often made her feel. When she'd finally left it all behind, she had sworn to herself that she would never go back to that kind of loneliness again.

She looked up at Dooley, noticing again how big he was, how strange it seemed for a man his size and breadth to be a chef. "Gregory tells me you're a chef. How did you ever get interested in cooking?" she asked curiously.

"It's a long story."

She smiled up at him. "We have two long blocks left to walk."

Dooley swept a hand through his hair, somehow managing not to dislodge the small piece of greenery. "I was fourteen years old when my dad left us and my mom had to go to work. Besides me, there were five kids, all of them under the age of eight years old. I quit school and became their surrogate mother."

There was no bitterness in his voice. But she had a feeling Dooley was the type of man who would never look back with regret or rancor. He would always have his energy, his gaze, focused on the future. "It must have been difficult for you," she replied.

He shrugged. "You do what has to be done when it comes to the welfare of your family." He smiled. "It certainly made me and my brothers and sisters un-usually close. Anyway," he continued, "I learned first to cook at home for the family, then when I was fif-teen I got a night job at Willie's Grill. It was owned by an old curmudgeon who had no family. When I was twenty, Willie died and, to my surprise, left the Grill to me." For the first time there was a touch of regret in his voice, a sense of great loss. "What about you? What's your story?"

"I don't have a story," Marina returned.

"Everyone has a story," he chided, his gaze warm on her. She was so achingly lovely, with part of her hair tumbling down, escaping the ponytail that had confined it earlier. The illumination from the street-lights played over her face, emphasizing each of her delicate features.

He wanted to know about her past, discover the essence of who she was. He wanted to connect with her, but sensed a reluctance on her part. Marina Burns had a built-in security system that kept her surrounded by an invisible shield. What she didn't realize was that Dooley could be extremely persistent when he thought the end result was worth it. And he had a feeling she was definitely worth an abundance of patience and persistence.

They had come to her apartment building, pausing out on the sidewalk. "Tell me about Mary Ann Rayburn," Dooley prompted, not wanting to let it go.

Marina heaved a tired sigh, half resenting his probing. "Mary Ann Rayburn grew up on a farm outside a tiny town in Arkansas. All she ever wanted was to move to New York City and become a famous actress. She's accomplished the first part, and she's working on the second."

"It's so important to you? To be famous?"

"It's the most important thing in my life," Marina replied fervently. "And I'm going to do it, too. It's just a matter of time. And nobody, nothing, can stop me." Her impassioned monologue was interrupted by

a young man who seemingly appeared from nowhere.
The wiry kid ran between Marina and Dooley, shoving Marina so hard she would have fallen had Dooley
not reached out to steady her.

"Are you all right?" he asked, his hand firm and
strong on her shoulder.

"Yes..." she replied, slightly disoriented, then
gasped in dismay. "Oh, Dooley, he grabbed my
purse."

Without hesitation, before Marina could even guess
his intent, Dooley took off after the culprit.
"Dooley...wait," she called after him, noticing the
athletic grace that moved him like the wind. "Dooley
James, you come back here," she yelled as he disappeared down a distant alley.

"Oh, that crazy, hick fool," she muttered, concern
for him flaring through her. Didn't he realize the kid
who grabbed her purse could have a weapon...maybe
a gun? Cold fingers of fear crawled up her spine.

Imagined news headlines flashed through her head:
Country Bumpkin Killed By Crazed Purse-Snatcher.
Southern Gentleman Sacrifices Life For Waitress's
Tips.

Oh, Dooley was going to get hurt and it was all her
fault.

Dooley ran effortlessly, his eyes never wavering
from the shadowlike figure of the purse-snatcher.
Dooley might be a country man, but he was wise in the
ways of the hunted, and anticipated the move that
took the kid into the dark alley on the left. He walked

into the alleyway cautiously. He assumed the kid didn't have a weapon, but he knew better than to bet his life on it.

Thankfully, the alley ended with a brick wall too high to scale. There, crouched in the darkness, Dooley could make out the kid. Dooley's heart constricted as he realized how young he was, probably no more than thirteen or fourteen. Where were his parents? Why did nobody seem to care that he was out on the streets in the middle of the night?

Dooley approached him slowly. "Look, kid, I don't want any problems. Just give me back the purse."

"Are you crazy, man?" The boy looked at Dooley with belligerence.

"No, I just want the purse. If you don't give it to me I'm going to get angry, then you'll really think I'm crazy."

The kid spit on the ground, as if to indicate his affection for Dooley.

Dooley sighed. He'd hoped he could scare the boy into giving up the purse, but it seemed something more physical was in order. With another deep sigh, Dooley moved forward.

Just as Marina was about to run and find him, he came back into her view, a jaunty grin on his face and her purse in his hand.

"Oh, Dooley." Relief propelled her forward and without thought she flew into his arms. For just a brief moment, his arms closed around her and she felt the solid strength of his embrace. "Oh, Dooley, that was a very foolish thing to do,'' she murmured into the front of his sweet-smelling shirt.

He grunted in reply and Marina stepped back, looking up at him. She was surprised to see that his forehead was dotted with little beads of perspiration, and his smile was not as jaunty as she'd first perceived. "Dooley, are you all right?"

"I'm fine," he said with a crooked grin. He handed her the purse. "I got it back before he managed to get anything out of it. But it seems that little coyote had a knife."

She stepped back and for the first time she realized he was holding his side, and the shirt beneath his open jacket was stained with blood. Marina sucked in her breath. "Oh, God, Dooley, you're hurt...we need to get you to the hospital...we need to call somebody, do something," she dithered, half-hysterical.

"Mary Ann, I'm fine," he said, his hand still pressed tightly against the wound. "I think it's just a graze."

"But it's bleeding so much." Marina took a deep breath. "I really think it needs to be looked at by a doctor."

"Heck, Mary Ann, I've cut and burned myself a hundred times in the kitchen and never went to a doctor. I'm not about to start changing my ways now." He attempted a grin, but his complexion was noticeably pale. "I'll just go home and clean this up," he said.

She knew she would never forgive herself if she allowed him to go to his apartment alone and then something happened to him. After all, he'd been stabbed while playing the knight in shining armor for her.

Decision made, she took him by the arm and tugged him toward her apartment building. "Come on, I can at least look at it, clean it up and see if you need stitches."

Once in her apartment, she directed him into the bathroom, where she instructed him to take off his shirt while she rummaged in the closet for a first-aid kit.

Marina found the kit and returned to the bathroom, pausing in the doorway, her breath catching in her throat as she looked at him. He sat on the edge of the bathtub, leaning over with his head resting against the porcelain wall. His eyes were closed and he held his wadded-up shirt tightly against his wound. But it was not the cut that captured Marina's immediate attention. It was the perfect symmetry of Dooley's chest that held her gaze.

Marina couldn't draw her way out of a paper bag, but at the moment she wished she were an artist and could capture the beauty of his exquisite proportions, the anatomy that displayed a muscular chest and a lean, taut stomach all covered with red-gold hair. She followed the pattern of fire-kissed curls down his broad chest to where a trail disappeared into the waistband of his slacks.

She suddenly remembered how he had looked in the restaurant, the hair peeking out from the front of his unbuttoned shirt looking like the dying embers of a fire in the candlelight. She'd wondered then—if she touched his chest, would it be warm? She now found herself wondering the same thing.

His eyes suddenly flew open and he grinned. "Are you okay?"

"Of course," she replied briskly, his voice effectively breaking the trance she'd momentarily fallen into. With studied efficiency, she set the first-aid kit on the sink and opened it, removing a bottle of peroxide and a handful of cotton. "The first thing we need to do is clean it."

He nodded, slowly taking the ruined shirt away from the gash. "I think the bleeding has almost stopped," he observed. The wound was on his side, just above his belt line.

Marina got down on her knees next to him, concentrating only on the task at hand. She didn't want to acknowledge that his skin was indeed warm, beckoning her fingers to linger and caress. She didn't want to think about the fact that for the first time in a very long time she felt the desire to be held in big, strong arms, she wanted to be kissed until she ached with need and she craved the abandonment that would come in fulfilling that need. She bit her bottom lip and concentrated on cleaning him up, shoving all other thoughts from her mind and hoping she wasn't hurting him.

The last thing Dooley focused on was pain. Instead, he concentrated on the light, caressing pressure of her fingers against his flesh, the way the tips of her hair danced erotically against him as she bent her head to get a closer view of the cut.

He could smell her, a soft, feminine scent that affected him more than anything he'd ever smelled before.

Without conscious thought, he reached out and placed a hand on her shoulder, wanting... no, *needing* to touch the smooth skin that beckoned him.

Her gaze fluttered up to his, a flush of vivid color on her cheeks. "Am I hurting you?"

He started to assure her that she was not, then realized that pain was the perfect excuse for his wayward hands to linger on the silken softness of her shoulder.

"Just a little," he said, grimacing slightly, his hand not moving from its position. "It's okay," he assured her.

Marina went back to work, acutely aware of his hand on her shoulder, creating a spreading warmth that swiftly moved through her entire body. "It doesn't look so deep," she said once she had the wound completely cleaned up. "I need to put some antiseptic on it." She grabbed another bottle from the first-aid kit. "This is going to sting," she warned him as she began to apply the medicine.

Dooley sucked in his breath, tightening not only the muscles of his chest and stomach, but his grip on her shoulder, as well.

Marina also had difficulty breathing as she saw the strength and beauty of his tightened muscles, felt the tautness beneath her fingertips.

She slapped gauze on the wound, then taped it up and stood up, needing to physically distance herself from him. She couldn't breathe when he was so close, couldn't think.

"That should hold you," she murmured, moving to the safety of the doorway, away from the aura of heat and light that seemed to emanate from his body.

Dooley picked up his suit jacket from the floor and followed her out of the bathroom. "Thanks for taking care of me," he said.

Marina shrugged, noticing how he seemed to fill her entire apartment with his presence. "It's the least I could do, especially since it was my purse you saved."

They both moved toward the door. "Mary Ann, I was wondering if perhaps you would help me tomorrow," he said, pausing, standing so close to her she had difficulty breathing.

"How can I help you?" she asked, her hand reaching up of its own volition to pluck the piece of lettuce from his hair. Soft...just as she'd thought it would be, his hair had the silky softness of expensive fur. How had he managed to chase down a criminal, get stabbed, and not dislodge the tenacious piece of lettuce? And why did his hair have to be so incredibly soft? Realizing where her thoughts were going, she stepped back and crossed her arms.

"Gregory might have told you, I'm in town to find a site for a new restaurant. I've got a real-estate agent working on it, but I'd really like to get out and scout a little on my own. The problem I'm having is that I know nothing about the city. I need a guide and I was wondering if you'd be available."

Her first impulse was to shout out a resounding no. She didn't want to spend any more time with Dooley James. He bothered her. He made her think of things that were in direct opposition to what she wanted out of life. Yet the practical side of her hesitated. Perhaps it would be best for her to help him, aid him in finding a site and getting back to South Carolina where he belonged. Once his business was completed, he would go home, where he would no longer be a distraction for her.

"I suppose I could help you for a day," she replied slowly.

"Great," he enthused. "Why don't I meet you here about eight in the morning."

Marina frowned. "Dooley, it's almost three o'clock now. Why don't we make it ten?"

"Okay," he agreed. For a moment he hesitated, and for one wild, crazy second, Marina was afraid he was going to kiss her.

She opened the door, then stepped backward, not quite meeting his eyes. She had a feeling if she looked into their green depths, she would be lost. She would be drawn into them, allow him to kiss her. And kissing Dooley was definitely something she didn't want to experience. She had a feeling it would be something she would never quite forget. "Good night, Dooley," she said faintly.

He hesitated another moment, then to her relief, he murmured good-night and left her apartment. Once he was gone, Marina locked the door, then sat down on the sofa and breathed a tremulous sigh.

What was wrong with her? What was it about Dooley that made her feel like it would be easy to forget her dreams of acting? What was it about him that made her remember she was a woman first, a struggling actress second?

Oh, she'd make sure she found him a site for his restaurant as quickly as possible. Hopefully, within the next couple of days, his business would be completed and he would wing his way back to the South, where his presence, his attractiveness, his magnetism couldn't touch her. She pulled herself up from the couch, somehow comforted by this thought.

She'd just lain down and turned out her light when she heard Dooley's voice drifting across the alley.

"Mary Ann," he yelled in a pseudo-whisper.

She sat up and looked outside, seeing his silhouette outlined in the window across the way.

"I'm really looking forward to tomorrow," he exclaimed.

"Yeah, so am I, so knock off the chitchat," a male voice growled from a nearby window.

Marina stifled a giggle, then waved to Dooley, acknowledging that she had heard him. She lay back down, staring at the patterns of light that danced on her ceiling, listening to sounds of the city streets outside. It was crazy—she was a city girl and Dooley was a country man. The city was where she belonged, where she wanted to be. Yet when she finally closed her eyes and began to drift to sleep, she imagined the sound of the wind rustling treetops and a low-throated frog croaking at the moon.

Chapter Five

She should never have agreed to accompany him, Marina thought the next morning as she got dressed. She should spend the day making the rounds, pounding the pavement, knocking on doors to find herself an acting job. She shouldn't be wasting her time with a man . . . any man. "And especially not Dooley," she muttered. She pulled on a sundress, knowing the heat of the day was going to be near intolerable.

She was in the middle of French-braiding her hair when Dooley knocked. He looked bright eyed and eager to go exploring the vast city.

"Have a seat," she instructed, moving back to the bathroom mirror. "I'll be ready to go in just a minute or two."

"Take your time," he replied agreeably, wandering around the small confines of the apartment with interest. She fascinated him, this woman with her Carolina sky-colored eyes and burst of long curly hair. He sensed a deep sadness in her, and he found it strange that he wanted to ease that sadness. He'd never felt this way about a woman before.

"How's your wound this morning?" Her voice drifted out of the bathroom.

"Fine, just a little sore," he answered, rubbing absently at the bandage on his side. He picked up a *Backstage* newspaper lying on the table, noticing the ads for auditions that were circled with red marker.

He'd always wondered about people who sought the limelight, people who had a need not to be loved by one, but by millions. Did Mary Ann really have the drive and ambition to achieve that particular dream? He really didn't know. She talked a good game, mouthed all the right words, but somehow Dooley didn't think she had the inner hardness that it took to survive the climb to the top. Of course, he could be wrong.

He set the newspaper down and moved over to the sofa, noticing a basket full of sewing items sitting on the floor. He picked up the thing that lay on top, an amused grin lifting the corners of his mouth. It was a stuffed mouse. What intrigued Dooley the most was that the mouse had red yarn hair and a matching beard. The creature wore a pair of denim slacks and a flannel shirt. The workmanship was exquisite, the doll delightful.

He still held the doll in his hands when she came out of the bathroom. "What's this?" he asked curiously, seeing the immediate flush of embarrassment sweep up her neck to color her cheeks.

"It's nothing," she murmured.

"But it looks like me," he observed.

"It's a voodoo doll," Marina exclaimed recklessly, irritated by his snooping. She snatched the mouse from his hands and threw it into the basket.

"Are you going to at least give me fair warning before you stick pins and needles into it?" His eyes were the color of spring, impish lights dancing there as his mouth curved upward teasingly.

Marina, realizing she'd overreacted, felt a responding smile on her own lips. "Actually, I lied, it's not a voodoo doll at all. I'm making it for Gregory's nephew."

She was grateful when he didn't pursue the topic and ask why the mouse had been made in his image. If he had, she wouldn't have had a reasonable answer. She refused to delve into the reasons that had prompted the mouse to be created in Dooley's likeness. She walked over to the door and looked at him expectantly. "Let's get this show on the road."

He nodded and followed her out the door.

"Do you have any idea where you want to go first?" she asked once they were outside on the sidewalk.

"I have a list of places from the real-estate agent."
He dug into the pocket of his well-worn jeans and
produced a folded sheet of paper. He straightened it
out and handed it to her.

Marina looked at the locations listed, mentally
forming a route to follow that would allow them to see
all the prospective sights in the shortest time possible.
The sooner Dooley found his restaurant, the sooner he
would leave her and New York behind.

"Can we walk to all these places?" Dooley asked as
they started off down the sidewalk.

"We could walk to a couple of them, but it will be
easier if we take the subway." She paused at a set of
stairs that led down.

His forehead wrinkled with uncertainty, his leaf
green eyes darkening noticeably. "The subway? I've
never ridden on one before."

"Then you're in for a real experience," Marina replied, taking his arm and pulling him down the stairs.

"I don't know about this...." Dooley said faintly
as she fed the appropriate tokens into the turnstile and
pushed him through. The platform was crowded with
people, but Dooley hung back, looking decidedly un-
comfortable. As the platform began trembling with
the approach of the train, his face blanched. "Mary
Ann, I can't do this," he said, taking a couple of steps
backward, away from the train that had just pulled to
a halt.

"Dooley, what's the matter?" Marina asked, wondering if the big man was ill.

"I can't ride on that," he explained, turning to walk back through the turnstile. He headed upward, toward the sunlight.

"But, Dooley, it's perfectly safe." Marina ran after him, finding it difficult to keep up with his broad, long strides. He reached the top step and breathed an audible sigh of relief.

He leaned against the railing and raised his face to the sun. "It's not natural," he said as Marina joined him. "I don't want some train carrying me down there in the bowels of the earth. If anything's going to happen to me, I want it to be up here, with the sun on my face and the sky overhead." His facial expression suddenly took on a look of vulnerability. "When I was nine years old, I fell down into an abandoned well. As I waited to be rescued, my biggest fear was that the sides would cave in and bury me alive." He smiled sheepishly. "I guess it left its mark." He shrugged, as if sloughing off the childhood memory. "We'll take a taxi."

Marina didn't object and was somehow touched by this show of vulnerability. It gave Dooley more depth, a new dimension, one that made him more appealing than ever.

However, as the day progressed, Marina was reminded again and again of how little she and Dooley really had in common. It was obvious he didn't like the city, with its constant activity and sense of frenzy. His face took on a distracted, slightly bewildered look, and he moved impatiently through the throngs of people that blocked their path no matter which way they decided to move.

But despite their differences, Marina found herself enjoying his sensitivity and his sense of humor. As he looked at the first site on their list, she listened as he voiced his objections to the location. "It's just not right," he said, standing at the front door of the closed-down restaurant. "The neighborhood isn't right."

"What's wrong with it?" Marina asked curiously. It seemed like a nice enough neighborhood to her.

"Look around. There are few children, very few elderly. It's obvious this is an area for young executives, yuppies. Those aren't the people who would frequent a home-style restaurant. They'll eat at salad bars and health-food places."

At each location Dooley found something wrong, his arguments making sense to Marina, who was surprised that beneath his good-old-boy persona, he had a keen business sense and a sharp eye for catching minute details. There was definitely more to Dooley James than met the eye, and what irritated her most was that she was intrigued by each piece of him she uncovered.

"I guess that's it," Marina exclaimed when they had viewed the last site on the list.

"Actually, there are a few more places I need to check out."

"Where?" she asked.

"Rockefeller Center," Dooley answered without hesitation.

Marina frowned. "You want to locate your restaurant around the Rockefeller Center?" She gazed at him skeptically. "Dooley, I don't mean to tell you how to run your business, but that's a pretty high dollar rent district for a little country restaurant."

He grinned. "Actually, going to the Rockefeller Center has nothing to do with business. I promised my mother I'd visit there, then tell her all about it when I get back home." His grin turned slightly sheepish. "In fact, there are several things here in the city I've been wanting to see, but didn't want to go alone."

Marina fought off a modicum of irritation. If he wanted to go sight-seeing, he should have hired a tour guide.

Still, she swallowed the irritation. After all, the day was already half-gone. There was nothing she had to do back at her apartment, and she had never been to Rockefeller Center. "Okay, let's go," she finally agreed, her words provoking another of Dooley's sunny smiles.

From Rockefeller Center, they walked across the street to St. Patrick's Cathedral, where Marina found herself as awed as Dooley by the magnificent example of Gothic architecture. From there, they went to the Museum of Modern Art, where they giggled like school kids as they tried to figure out what was depicted by some of the paintings and sculptures.

For lunch, they went to a trendy little restaurant with a view of Central Park. The prices were obscene, but the food was absolutely magnificent.

"That sure beat boxed macaroni and cheese," Marina exclaimed as she pushed her empty plate away from her.

"It was good," Dooley agreed. "How about some dessert?"

"Oh, no, I couldn't eat another bite," she protested. "But you go ahead."

"I think I'll try the rum cake," he replied, giving his order to the waitress.

"I know why you decided to become a chef," Marina said with a small smile. "Because you love to eat."

He smiled. "Next to cooking, eating is the thing I do best." He looked at her curiously. "So, tell me, what made you decide to become an actress?"

"It's just something I've always wanted to do for as long as I can remember."

"Did your parents encourage you?"

She shook her head. "My parents died when I was very young. I was raised by my aunt and uncle, and they didn't encourage or discourage me."

He looked at her intently, wondering why it was that whenever he tried to learn something about her personal life, she closed down, withdrew. It wasn't anything overt, rather it was merely a distance in the blueness of her eyes, a tightening of her facial muscles.

He leaned forward and placed a hand over hers, a smile touching his lips. "I'll bet you led those Arkansas fellows on quite a chase."

She laughed. "Not really. I was skinny and shy, and lived too far out of town to have any real friends or 'fellows.'" Her smile slowly fell from her mouth, and her eyes once again took on the distant look Dooley had begun to expect. "Actually, that's why I started sewing my little mouse friends."

Dooley tightened his grip on her hand, recognizing the loneliness of a little girl who'd made her own friends from bits of scrap material. Dooley, with his large family, had never known the pangs of loneliness, at least not as a child. It had only been lately that he'd felt the need to connect with somebody, the desire for a wife and his own family.

Still, more than anything, at the moment he wished he could absorb the pain he suspected lay hidden in her heart. Again he was surprised at how something about Mary Ann evoked a protectiveness in him, a desire to shield her from the unhappiness the world sometimes offered.

"I've been thinking," he said, his thumb making small circles on the back of her hand. "For some time I've been thinking about adding a little gift area to my restaurants, but so far I haven't come across anything that I'd be interested in selling. That is, until today."

"Today?" Marina looked at him curiously, thinking back over what they had seen while sight-seeing that might have interested him.

He nodded. "Your mice. They are exactly the sort of items I'm looking for."

"That's crazy," Marina protested, a warm flush of pleasure rising up in her despite her own words of protest. "They're just silly little dolls."

Dooley shook his head. "They're whimsical, homemade, bewitching creatures, and they would be an asset to my restaurants. Did you design them?"

She nodded. "Yes, but they're just dolls I make in my spare time, for relaxation."

"I'd like to put them in my restaurants. Think about it, that's all I'm asking."

Before she had time to answer, the waitress returned with his dessert, and he reluctantly released her hand.

Marina was grateful for the break in physical contact. His hand felt too comfortable wrapped around hers like a glove. It had given her a strange sort of security and comfort, one she hadn't realized she needed until now. She was also confused by the business proposition he'd just made her. There was something appealing about it and at the same time repugnant. She'd begun making those mice long ago—wouldn't returning to selling them now be a sign of moving backward instead of ahead?

"Tell me about your brothers and sisters," she said suddenly, wanting to steer the conversation away from her personal life and ancient history. She'd come a long way from that lonely childhood and had promised herself she would never go back, not even through memories. "Are they all red-haired like you?"

Dooley smiled, obviously pleased by thoughts of his family. "No, I'm the only copper kettle, as my mother says. The rest of them are blond. The oldest is Kate. She's twenty-three, married and has two kids. Then there's Jimmy, he's twenty-one and owns his own construction company. Next are John and Billy, they both work for Jimmy. Finally there's Jenny, who's a high school junior."

"You're especially close to Jenny," Marina observed, noticing the way his voice softened, lingered over the girl's name. She found herself wondering how it would be to hear that same adoring, caressing tone when he said her own name.

He nodded, his sensual lips curving into a smile. "Yeah, Jenny's a peach. She's constantly mothering me, telling me I should be married and have a dozen kids of my own."

"Is that what you want?" Marina asked curiously.

"Sure," he answered without hesitation. "I want to wake up in the cool Carolina mornings with a woman lying next to me. I want to go to work and think about her all day long, hurry back home to her. I want somebody there for me, sharing my life with me."

The image was evocative, creating in Marina a feeling of mourning for dreams long dead, desires nearly forgotten. "That's not for me," she laughed nervously, consciously pushing the strange feeling out of her mind. "I want the smell of greasepaint in my nose, the heat that comes from a spotlight on my face. I want standing ovations, the sound of applause."

"And nobody to share it with?" he asked curiously, taking a bite of his rum cake.

"Perhaps someday," she answered, shrugging her shoulders as if she didn't care one way or the other. "But not for a very long time. I need to focus all my energies, all my attention on attaining my goals." She twirled her half-empty water glass thoughtfully between her hands, as Dooley ate his cake, seemingly lost in thoughts of his own.

Sure, his words had painted a pretty picture, but what he'd described would never be enough for her. She had a desire too strong, a well of need too deep inside her to compromise her dreams.

"That was wonderful," Dooley announced, the last bite of rum cake on his fork. He extended it across the table to her. "Here . . . just a bite. . . ."

Rather than protest, Marina opened her mouth, taking the rich cake off the tines of the fork. It seemed an intimate thing to do, eating off the same utensil he'd used. He furthered the intimacy by reaching out and brushing a crumb from her cheek, his hand lingering a moment longer than necessary.

Marina flushed with warmth and moved back in her chair. "So, now that you've refueled, are you ready to continue the exploration of this vast city?"

He nodded, left money for the meal and the tip, then together they left the restaurant. From there they walked to Central Park, where Dooley insisted they both take off their shoes and socks and enjoy the trickle of the lush grass against their bare feet.

"Since I've been here in the city, this is what I've missed," Dooley said as they carried their shoes over to a tree and sat down in the shade. "There's nothing that sets the world right like the feel of the warm earth beneath a man's feet and the sweet smell of grass in his nose."

"You should have been a farmer," she observed, finding the shade pleasant relief from the hot sun.

"I do a little farming now. A couple of months ago, I bought a big old plantation house with about fifty acres." He smiled, that warm, pleasant one that made a funny catch in Marina's throat. "I call the place Whispering Pines because it's surrounded by big pine trees, but my family calls it Dooley's Folly, because the place needs a whole lot of work."

"How are you ever going to find the time to work on a house, do a little farming, and still run your restaurants?"

He shrugged his broad shoulders. "The five restaurants require very little from me. I've got good people working for me and they pretty well run themselves. I check in every couple of weeks or so to make sure everything is okay, but basically my managers take care of the day-to-day operation. As far as the work on the house goes, if you buy a house that needs work, it helps to have a few brothers in the construction business."

"What about the new restaurant here? Won't it require a lot of time and energy?"

"A little, but I have a lot of people who do a lot of the work for me. It should only take a couple of months to get things under control."

"Then what?" Marina asked, wondering what direction life would take Dooley James. He'd already accomplished so much, overcome what some would have called a harsh, miserable childhood. Somehow, she had a feeling life wouldn't take Dooley anywhere, he would take life for a ride.

"Then . . . who knows," he answered. "There are a million things I'd like to do . . . starting with that." He pointed across the park, where horse-drawn carriages stood ready for hire. He jumped up with a grace and agility that belied his size. "Come on," he urged with a wide grin. He held out his hand to help her up, noticing how her hair gleamed in the sunlight that danced through the leaves of the trees overhead. The heat had brought out her freckles, making them visible across the bridge of her nose. The peach-colored sundress she wore emphasized her exquisite shape and the creamy tones of her skin. Dooley thought she was the loveliest woman he'd ever seen.

As they walked, he thought back over their recent conversation. She had told him very little about herself; her eyes and facial expression had spoken more than her words.

What Dooley hadn't told her was that he'd spent most of his life thus far striving for success in his business; now he was ready to focus on the challenge of his personal life. And the more time he spent with her, the more he wondered if perhaps she was the woman he wanted as part of his personal life.

He smiled at her and caught her hand as they approached the carriages.

Marina returned his smile, wondering what it was about him that made her feel so good, and yet somewhat frightened at the same time. She'd enjoyed the day, found his enthusiasm contagious, his smiles and light touches addictive. She sensed a gentleness in him, a tenderness that was very appealing, but she could also remember the fire that had lit his eyes when he'd thought the drunk in the restaurant had overstepped the boundaries with her.

As Dooley made the arrangements with the driver, she got up into the carriage and sank down into the luxurious leather seat.

He joined her, his arm around her shoulders, his warm thigh pressed provocatively against her own.

"Ah, this is nice," he murmured as the driver clucked his tongue and the carriage moved forward.

"I've never ridden in one of these before," Marina told him, enjoying the gentle sway of the carriage, Dooley's subtle scent settling all around her. "I've never been to the Rockefeller Center or St. Patrick's before today, either."

"And I'll bet you're one of those New Yorkers who has never been to the Statue of Liberty," he chided teasingly, catching a strand of her hair between his fingers.

"You'd win the bet," she admitted. "The people who live here don't take the time to sightsee. It's the tourists who enjoy the sights." When she'd first arrived in New York, she had been so desperate to fit in, to become a New Yorker, that she didn't want to do anything that would classify her as a mere tourist. Now she was sorry she hadn't seen much of what the city had to offer.

She leaned her head back against the seat and closed her eyes, enjoying the heat, the clippity-clop of the horses' hooves and the gentle tickling of Dooley's hand dancing in the hair that had escaped from the braid.

He would be a good lover—the thought jumped into her mind unbidden. He would be gentle and patient, bringing with him the lust for life that was such an intrinsic part of him. It was a seductive thought, causing her to feel as though the sun overhead had somehow relocated itself in the pit of her stomach.

It was a familiar heat, one that had begun the night before as she had admired the perfection of Dooley's chest. She'd been fighting against it all day, but now, with his breath warm against her neck, his fingers weaving magic in her hair, the sun reached its zenith and the heat was too intense to fight.

She sensed his face moving closer to hers, knew his lips were only a whisper away.

"Mary Ann."

Her name was a sigh escaping from him, beckoning her to open her eyes and look at him.

She did, and she saw the emerald fire of his eyes, mirroring the heat that coiled inside her. She knew he was going to kiss her, and she wanted the kiss. His mouth covered hers gently, as if experimenting with the taste and shape of her lips.

He shifted position so that both his arms enveloped her, pulling her chest against the hard solidness of his own. At the same time he deepened the kiss, his tongue moving to introduce itself to hers.

For a long moment Marina's brain went into a holding pattern, not thinking, not considering consequences, rather simply existing on a plane where there were no thoughts, only tactile pleasures.

She'd never been kissed by a man with a beard before and she found the soft rub of whiskers strangely erotic. Also erotic was the play of his hands, first tangling in her hair, then moving across her back in slow, exquisite caresses that caused her to unconsciously arch her back and moan into his mouth.

"Another time around?" The driver spoke without turning around in his seat.

"Sure," Dooley answered, his lips moving to reclaim Marina's.

The words penetrated the fog in Marina's head, making thought possible once again. "No," she protested, moving out of Dooley's arms. "I've really got to get home," she said, a blush covering her cheeks as she saw the curious look in his eyes.

She was grateful that he didn't argue with her. He remained silent as they rode in a taxi back to her apartment.

His silence didn't bother her; she was too busy talking to herself. *What did you think you were doing?* she fumed inwardly, angry that she had allowed herself the momentary weakness of the kiss. The very last thing she needed in her life was a man. She didn't want to split her focus, splinter the drive she knew it took to succeed in the area she'd chosen for herself. She'd seen it happen to other women who'd sacrificed their stardom for the love of a man, and she wasn't about to make the same mistake.

Besides, Dooley was the worst possible choice for a relationship. Eventually he'd go back to South Carolina, back to his Whispering Pines. He belonged to the country just as she belonged to the city.

She breathed a sigh of relief as the taxi pulled up in front of her apartment building. "I'm sorry to cut the day short, but I'm baby-sitting tonight and I've got some cleaning to do before the kids arrive," she babbled as he walked with her to her apartment door. "Thanks for lunch and everything. It was a pleasant day," she continued as she dug her key out of her purse and unlocked her door. "Well..." She turned and smiled at him brightly. "I guess I'll see you some other time."

Without a word, he pushed past her and into the apartment. His eyes were the dark green of jade, and he suddenly looked menacingly big. "You didn't really think you were going to get away so easily," he said. He closed the apartment door, then turned to face her.

Chapter Six

Marina felt her heart jump up in her throat. Had she misjudged Dooley James? Was he really some crazy hillbilly ax-murderer? "What...what do you mean?" she asked, surprised that her throat was unnaturally dry.

Dooley walked across the room and placed his hands on her shoulders. "Don't look at me like that," he chided softly, instantly dispelling the momentary fear she'd felt.

Instead, she once again felt the same heat that had overtaken her in the carriage. Dooley's hands were warm on her shoulders, evoking the stirring fire of desire deep inside her.

No, if Dooley was going to harm her, he wouldn't do it with an ax—he'd kill her dreams with the softness of his gaze, devastate her with the heat of his caresses.

"Dooley..." she murmured, taking a step back from him in an attempt to escape the killing pleasure of his nearness.

"You can't give a man a toe-curling kiss, then just pretend it didn't happen," he admonished, his hands moving so that his thumbs now rubbed in small sensual circles across the top of her collarbones. The green of his eyes emitted a hypnotic warm depth that Marina found herself falling into, unable to stop the headlong plunge that made time stand still, the room dim as Dooley's lips touched hers once again.

He wrapped her in a cocoon of security, his big strong arms feeling like a comfortable coat warding off the cold of the world. He was an anchor in a tumultuous sea, a haven against a host of insecurities and doubts. How easy it would be to allow him to sweep her away from the uncertainties of her life. How easy it would be to forget her dreams of a life on the stage. How simple it would be to fall in love with him.

She jerked away from him, moving back so that not even his outstretched arms could touch her. "Dooley, you've got to stop kissing me," she said, her cheeks flushed with color.

"If I'm not mistaken, you were doing a pretty good job of kissing me back," he said with a small smile.

"Well, we've got to stop."

"Why? We do it so well." Dooley's gaze caressed her, noting the high color of her cheeks, the haze of desire that changed her eyes from their azure shade to a midnight blue. At the moment, more than anything, Dooley wanted to sweep her up in his arms, carry her over to the couch and make love to her. He could see her breasts pushing against the fabric of her sundress with each of her breaths and never had he wanted a woman like he did her at this very moment. He wanted to kiss every freckle on the end of her nose, taste the sweetness of her naked flesh, feel the warmth of her curves pressed tightly against his own.

"Stop looking at me like that," Marina exclaimed.

"Like what?"

The blush on her cheeks deepened. "Like I'm a piece of rum cake you want to taste."

Dooley's grin widened. "Now that's an interesting concept."

"Dooley, I'm serious." Her tone held a note of desperation. She began to pace across the living room floor. "I've told you since the moment we met what I want to do with the rest of my life."

Dooley nodded, appreciating the way her sundress emphasized the graceful fluidity of her body as she moved across the floor.

"I'm not looking for any personal relationships. I've told you all along what I want."

He nodded again. "A life on the stage, but isn't it possible you might want other things for yourself, as well?"

Marina shook her head. "I want to be an actress. That's all I want and that's all I need," she returned fervently, stopping her pacing and facing him once again. "I'm going to be an actress, and I can't waste my time seeing the sights of the city or kissing a man who has no place in my future plans. Do you understand?"

"I understand," he replied solemnly. "I promise I won't ask you to go sight-seeing again. But I can't promise you that I won't kiss you again if the opportunity presents itself." Before she had a chance to respond or protest, Dooley walked out of the apartment.

A lighthearted tune escaped his lips in the form of a whistle as he walked toward his own apartment building. Her words warning him off, telling him there was no hope for a relationship between them, didn't bother him. Her mouth had said the words, but her eyes, her kiss, had told a much different story. She'd responded to him eagerly, hungrily. It had been more than just a mere physical response. He'd felt her soul reaching out to make contact with his own. Yes, she'd warned him off with words, but he knew he'd touched her someplace deep within.

There was a loneliness in her eyes, a love that remained untapped in her heart. He wanted to be the man to banish the loneliness. He wanted to be the one to tap into the well of emotion she tried to deny.

She professed to want a life on the stage, the adulation of thousands of strangers. But Dooley hoped that someplace deep in her soul, Mary Ann Rayburn wanted something much different. He hoped what she wanted was the adulation and adoration of just one man. All he had to do was be patient and, hopefully, eventually she would realize exactly what it was she wanted. He hoped it wasn't just wishful thinking on his part.

"I know exactly what I want," Marina said as she and Gregory walked down the sidewalk toward the small off-Broadway theater where auditions were to take place within the hour. "I want a part in this play. Any part—it doesn't have to be the lead, or a supporting role. I'd settle for a small walk-on, just a validation that my dreams of becoming an actress aren't beyond my reach." She looked at Gregory with frustration. "I've been working at this for the past year, and I've gotten nothing for my efforts."

"I'm beginning to wonder if I'm not getting too old for this line of work," Gregory said, his voice more subdued than usual.

Marina suddenly realized he'd been unusually quiet all morning. She now looked at him curiously. "Gregory, is something wrong?" She grabbed his arm and linked hers through it.

"No, why?"

"It's not like you to talk such nonsense about being too old for this business. You're always the one who perks me up when I get depressed."

He gave her a small grin. "I guess my perk is pooped," he said, making Marina laugh.

She gave him a sly grin. "I guess I'd be pretty tired too, if I had stayed out until all hours of the morning with Josie."

Gregory shook his head thoughtfully. "She's the most irritating woman I've ever known. Somehow she talked me into helping her move furniture last night, and I thought before I got done I'd pull all my hair out." He paused a moment, then continued. "She's a slob, she's undisciplined, she sings through her nose, and her kids are terrors."

"So why did you agree to help her?"

He shrugged. "That's what I've been trying to figure out for the last several hours."

"It couldn't be because you like her?"

Gregory didn't answer.

Marina took his silence as a positive sign. She clapped her hands together in delight. "Oh, Gregory, that's wonderful. You really like her?"

"I shouldn't like her. She's everything I don't want. She represents everything I swore I'd never have, but when she smiles at me, she makes me feel funny." He shook his head once again, as if unable to believe his own feelings.

"Well, I think it's terrific," Marina exclaimed. "I'd love to see my two best friends find happiness together."

"Don't go shoving me toward the altar. All I'm saying is that she might not be as bad as I thought she was." He looked at her sideways. "What about you?

When are you going to find somebody to be happy with?"

"I don't need anyone," Marina scoffed.

"I sort of thought that you and Dooley..." His voice trailed off as she looked at him irritably.

"That Dooley and I would what? Get together? Have a relationship? That's the most ridiculous thing I've ever heard."

"What's so ridiculous about it? Dooley's a terrific guy, and I think he's quite taken with you. He told me about you taking him sight-seeing the other day."

"Dooley and I want very different things out of life," Marina answered, trying not to think about how wonderful it had felt to be held in his strong arms, trying to forget the taste of his lips, the erotic whisper of his beard against her chin.

Utter foolishness. It was crazy to even think that she and Dooley could ever have a relationship. Dooley was a country man, and Marina had left the country far behind. She was a city girl whose first priority was her career. He'd want a woman whose first priority was family and home. It was a jarring picture that offered no solution, no hope for the future.

"It would be foolish for Dooley and me to try to have any kind of a relationship. It would only end in heartache for one of us," she exclaimed.

Gregory was silent for a long moment. "I just want you to be happy, Marina," he finally said.

"I will be happy if I get a part in this play," she announced as they came to the small theater. "Now, let's go in there and knock them dead."

The audition lasted three grueling hours, but at the end of those hours, Marina was ecstatic. She'd gotten a part.

"Congratulations, kid," Gregory said, giving her a hug before they started walking back to their apartment building.

"I still can't believe it," Marina replied, excitement dancing around in her stomach like a hyperactive child. She frowned at Gregory and hugged him again. "I just wish you would have gotten a role, too. It would have been great if both of us could have been in the play."

Gregory shrugged. "It just wasn't in the cards for me." He smiled at her. "But it's a beginning for you. You're on your way."

Marina sighed happily, still unable to believe her luck. "It's an awfully small part, but you're right. It's a beginning." She danced up the sidewalk, unable to contain her excitement.

Gregory followed after her, an indulgent grin on his face. "Enjoy it, kid. Unfortunately, most of these off-Broadway productions don't last long."

"At least this will be something to put on my résumé for when I have to audition again."

"Ms. Burns, may I have your autograph?" Gregory teased.

"Oh, please, I'm too famous to give autographs," Marina replied with mock hauteur that quickly dissolved into laughter.

"Just don't quit your job yet," Gregory warned.

"Don't worry." Marina laughed. "I'm not going to do anything crazy. The play won't pay enough for me to quit waitressing. But I'm going to have to talk to the boss about changing my hours. We start rehearsals next week." She shivered, imagining her name in lights on a marquee, the sound of applause ringing in her ears.

It was an image that remained with her for the duration of the walk home. As they rounded the corner near their apartment building, they met Dooley. He stood at the newsstand buying a newspaper.

As always, Marina felt a small catch in her chest at the sight of him. She suddenly realized that in the space of only a couple of days, she'd begun to look at him as a friend, and she wanted to share her news with him.

"Dooley." She raced toward him. "I got a part in a play," she announced, unable to contain her excitement.

"Hey, that's great," he exclaimed, lifting her up in a bear hug of congratulations.

He held her to him a moment longer than necessary and she could smell the sunshine freshness of him, feel the beat of his heart against her own. When he finally released her, setting her back down onto the sidewalk, she felt giddy.

It's the excitement of the part, she told herself. *It has nothing to do with the feel of his arms around me.*

"What about you? Did you get a part, too?" Dooley asked Gregory.

"Not this time. Today was Marina's day," Gregory said with a fond smile at her.

"We should celebrate," Dooley said. "I've got a bottle of champagne at my place. Why don't the two of you come on up and we'll toast Mary Ann's lucky day."

"Why not," Gregory agreed.

"Why not," Marina echoed recklessly.

Together the three of them headed for the apartment Dooley called home for the duration of his stay in New York.

"The fellow who owns this place is in Europe on an assignment," he explained as he unlocked the door and ushered them inside. "My secretary knows how much I dislike staying in hotels, so she arranged for me to sublet this while I'm here."

"He must be a photographer," Marina observed, admiring the many still shots that decorated the walls. Most of them were photographs of the city, some disturbing in their black-and-white reality. Others were brilliant color photos of flowers and birds.

Dooley nodded and went to the refrigerator to get the champagne.

"It's a nice little place," Gregory said, sitting down onto the overstuffed sofa.

Marina nodded her agreement and walked over to the window, surprised at the perfect view he had into her apartment across the alleyway. His window was a foot higher than hers, giving him an unobstructed, clear vantage point of her place. She needed to be more vigilant in closing her shades, she reminded herself.

"Here we are." Dooley set three goblets on the coffee table and poured a healthy amount of bubbly in each. After he'd finished, they each picked up a glass.

"To Mary Ann," Dooley toasted, his gaze warm as he smiled at her. "May all your dreams come true." He turned to Gregory. "And to you, Gregory. May your luck change at the next audition."

"I could use a change of luck," Gregory retorted. They drank, Marina laughing with delight as the bubbles tickled her nose. She felt Dooley's gaze on her and looked up to find him studying her intently. Warmth suffused her face and she quickly looked away, wondering what it was about him that so discomfited her. What was it about him that made her feel half-breathless? What was it about him that made her feel a vague sense of anticipation?

"Cheese," Dooley said suddenly. "Nothing goes better with champagne than a little Brie." He turned to the refrigerator and grabbed the cheese.

As he arranged the snacks on a platter, he listened absently to Gregory's inane chatter, but all his attention was focused on Marina, who had moved back over to the window.

God, she was beautiful. When she'd come running up to him outside on the sidewalk, the sun glinting in her hair and the radiant smile on her face, his want for her had been a physical ache in the pit of his stomach.

Her eyes had shone with an inner glow, and for a split second, he'd hoped it had been the sight of him that had put the glow in her eyes, the smile on her face. But no, it had been the thrill of success, the excitement of getting the part, and Dooley felt a curious bereavement, wondering if he could ever inspire that look on her face.

"I've got an announcement to make." Gregory's sober tone captured Dooley's attention. He carried the cheese and crackers over to the coffee table and joined Gregory on the sofa. Marina turned from the window and looked at her friend curiously.

"Marina, while I was hanging around this afternoon to see how you were going to do at the audition, I came to a decision." He paused a long moment, as if finding the words difficult to say. "I'm not going to audition for any more parts. I'm getting out of show business."

Marina stared at him in horror. "You aren't serious?"

He nodded. "I'm very serious."

"What are you planning to do?" Dooley asked curiously.

"I'm not sure. I took some business courses a couple years ago, you know, as a backup. Maybe it's time I put some of that particular knowledge to use."

"You're giving up," Marina exclaimed, looking at Gregory incredulously. The champagne she'd just sipped turned sour in her stomach. "How can you even think about not being an actor?"

"I've been thinking about it for the past couple of months. Never knowing when my next job is going to be, never knowing how the rent is going to get paid…it was okay for a long while, but now I'm tired of the vagabond existence. I want some stability in my life."

"But it's what you've dreamed about for so long," she protested, unable to understand his decision to quit acting.

"Maybe Gregory's dreams have changed," Dooley interjected. Gregory shot the big man a grateful look, but Marina glared at Dooley.

"You're just disappointed because you didn't get a part today. You'll feel differently tomorrow," she said in desperation.

Gregory shook his head. "I don't think so. And I'm not giving up, I'm just changing my goals."

"You're letting go of your dreams," Marina retorted, unsure why she was so angry, almost frightened by Gregory's decision to quit acting. "You're settling for less than you want."

"Mary Ann, a man has a right to change his dreams, decide his own future," Dooley said softly. "Maybe Gregory's just grown some. Now his needs and desires have changed into something different."

"That's exactly right," Gregory returned, again looking at Dooley with thankfulness.

"Have you ever considered the restaurant business?" Dooley asked.

Gregory shrugged his shoulders. "I'm open to all suggestions. Why?"

"I'm soon going to be looking for somebody to manage my place here in the city. If you have some business training, maybe we should talk."

"I'd like that," Gregory replied.

"This is crazy," Marina said. "Gregory, you can't do this to me."

"He's not doing anything to you, Mary Ann," Dooley said softly.

"My name is Marina. Why do you persist in calling me Mary Ann?" she yelled back, not knowing what was the cause of her anger, but suddenly it was there, choking her. "And what do you know about any of this?" She glared at Dooley. "You're just a country bumpkin fresh from South Carolina. What do you know about anything?" She turned back to look at her friend. "Gregory, you're making a big mistake. Take some time to think this over. Don't make a decision that's eventually going to make you unhappy." She turned back to Dooley. "And why don't you go back to South Carolina where you belong?" For a moment her words hung in the air, and the men stared at her in surprise. Then, with her anger still churning in her stomach, she stormed out of the apartment.

Her angry footsteps carried her quickly to her own apartment, where she flipped her shades closed, not wanting to look out and see the two men in the apartment across the alley.

Gregory and his stupid decision to stop acting, and Dooley supporting him, agreeing that his decision was sound—they were both crazy. Gregory probably would have changed his mind and forgotten the whole crazy idea of quitting acting if Dooley had kept his mouth shut. Instead, he'd practically handed Gregory a job. Oh, why had Dooley messed everything up? A lot of help he had been in the entire situation. Why couldn't he just stay out of it? What did he understand about the needs and desires of actors?

She thought again of Dooley and Gregory. Oh, she could throttle the both of them. She flopped down onto the sofa, her stomach sick with churning emotions. Gregory, no longer an actor? It didn't seem possible.

She and Gregory were a team, two struggling actors working to make it big. How could he just turn his back on what he loved? How could he turn his back on his dreams? Gregory's decision suddenly made Marina feel vulnerable as she realized how easily dreams could be discarded.

She leaned forward, her hands covering her face, and took a few deep, cleansing breaths, trying to get a handle on the emotions that swirled around inside her.

Almost immediately the anger flowed out of her, and instead shame slowly crept over her. She'd acted like a spoiled child. Gregory had told her his decision, looking for support and friendship, and instead she had yelled at him like a fishwife.

She now recognized the emotion that pulled at her, one she had masked with her anger: fear. For the last year, Gregory had been her strength; he'd been the one to help her brush herself off and try again when she'd failed at yet another audition. They had been comrades working to succeed in the crazy world of the theater.

It frightened her, how easily he'd made the decision to turn his back on his acting career for a more conventional job. Gregory had been every bit as determined as Marina to succeed in the theater, yet he'd easily changed his mind.

She curled up on the sofa and wrapped her arms around herself. She had never felt so alone as she did at this moment.

Chapter Seven

"Are you still mad at me?" Gregory asked, peeking his head into Marina's apartment early the next morning.

"I should be asking you if you're mad at me," Marina replied with an apologetic smile. She motioned for him to join her at the small kitchen table. When he was seated across from her she reached out and took his hands in hers. "I spent a miserable night, tossing and turning, listening to my conscience and a lot of self-recriminations. I behaved badly last night, and I apologize." She released his hands and got up to pour him a cup of coffee.

"Marina, you know how crazy this profession is. I've been working, waiting for my big break for the past ten years. I've just decided it's time to face the

reality that I may never make it big in this business."
He nodded his thanks as she set the cup of brew before him, then he continued. "I want a job that will provide some kind of security for my old age."

"Gregory, you're a long way from old age," Marina scoffed.

"Still, I don't want to suddenly wake up one day and find myself an old man and realize that while I was busy pursuing unrealistic dreams, life passed me by."

"If that's truly what you want, then I'm happy for you."

She smiled at him with a touch of sadness, knowing their lives were taking paths that would eventually carry them away from each other. No longer were they two friends working toward common goals, no longer were they two against the world. Gregory now had a different path to follow, and Marina...she clung tighter than ever to her dreams of one day becoming a famous actress.

"So, what's on your agenda for today?" Gregory asked, cutting through her somewhat morose thoughts.

"I need to go to the restaurant this afternoon and see about changing my hours. Most of my rehearsals are going to be in the evenings, so I'll see if I can work lunch shifts at the restaurant." She frowned. "I also need to talk to Josie. I'm afraid I'm going to have a conflict between baby-sitting Robert and Susan and the play rehearsals."

"Don't worry, I'll help Josie with the kids." He grinned sheepishly at her look of surprise. "Don't look so shocked. I still think Robert needs a firm hand, but I'll help out in the interest of furthering your career and keeping the rest of us in this apartment safe from an unattended Robert."

Marina laughed. "What a gallant offer. I appreciate it."

Gregory's smile slowly sobered and he looked at her slyly. "I know something else you might consider doing today."

"What's that?" she asked curiously.

"You might say a few kind words to my favorite 'country bumpkin.' You were a little rough on him yesterday."

Marina flushed, remembering her sharp, harsh words to Dooley. "Yes, I do owe him an apology." Although for some reason it felt more comfortable to maintain anger toward him. The anger felt like a sturdy shield, ready to fend off other, more disturbing emotions that the big man evoked in her. But he had done nothing to deserve her ire. He'd simply been reasoning with her, trying to make her see Gregory's side of the issue. No, he hadn't deserved her spiteful words and she did owe him an apology. "I'll talk to him today," she told Gregory.

But somehow the hours of the day slipped by with no opportunity to talk to Dooley. By the time she finished working out her schedule with her boss at the restaurant, it was after noon. Realizing she hadn't eaten anything all morning, she bought a hot dog from a corner vendor and took it to a small neighborhood park.

Once there, she sat down on one of the park benches and ate slowly, enjoying the country ambience the park afforded. In the past year of living in New York City, she'd forgotten how much she'd loved the sight of the green hills, the scent of wildflowers, the feel of grass tickling the bottoms of her feet.

It had taken Dooley to remind her of the good memories of her youth. Dooley, with his mountain-pine scent, his sun-browned skin, his soft Southern drawl, had made her remember the many mornings she'd awakened to the cool, fresh air and wished there were somebody lying beside her who would wrap his sleep-warmed arms around her, cuddle her against his heart.

The disturbing thing was that now, when she imagined that scene, it was always Dooley lying next to her in the bed, holding her against him, making love to her until she cried out in exquisite pleasure.

In fact, it seemed that every time she saw Dooley, every time he crossed through her thoughts, she remembered the magnificent physique of his bare chest, the feel of his lips on hers. And unfortunately, these thoughts were crossing into her mind far too often for comfort. What was more, her imagination was beginning to fill her head with pictures of what might have happened had she not stopped their kissing the night of their sight-seeing.

She polished off her hot dog and stood up. She had more important things to do than sit and indulge herself in fantasies of a man who would most likely be gone in the next couple of weeks. Dooley would go back to South Carolina and marry some homespun woman who wanted nothing more than to love and be loved by him. And as for Marina Burns? She was on her way to stardom.

All day long Dooley half hoped, half expected Marina to stop by his apartment and apologize for her heated words of the night before. He had confidence that once the shock of Gregory's announcement wore off, she would recognize that she'd responded with anger, but had actually been frightened. He'd recognized the fear in her eyes, smelled it emanating from her.

It was a look, a scent he recognized from an incident in his past. He'd been about sixteen years old and was out hunting with a bunch of his high school buddies. He'd spotted a doe and moved in for a better shot. Before he could pull the trigger, the breeze changed direction and the doe got a whiff of Dooley's human smell. Dooley knew the instant it happened; the doe's soft brown eyes widened and he smelled the animal's fear. In a split-second decision, Dooley lowered his gun and allowed the deer to bound off into the nearby cover of brush. It had been the first and the last time Dooley had gone hunting.

Yes, he'd recognized Marina's fear. What he didn't understand was what caused it. And what he wanted to know more than anything was how he could assuage it. He couldn't stand the hurt bewilderment that had been in her eyes. He'd hated to see the fear radiating from her, and the discovery made him aware he was becoming more emotionally tied to Marina than he'd realized.

He now got up off the sofa where he'd been lounging and walked to the window. He moved aside the sheer curtain, noting the smell of old garbage and burning rubber mingling with stale cooking scents.

Dusk was falling, but the beauty of twilight was muted by the smoke in the air, the hundreds of streetlights that interfered. New York City might be fine for some folks, but Dooley knew with a certainty that if he were to stay here for too long, he would wither and die.

Without thought, his gaze traveled across the alley, directly into Marina's apartment window. She was there, sitting on the sofa, reading a piece of paper she held in her hand. For a moment, Dooley allowed himself the pleasure of simply admiring the curve of her cheek, the graceful length of her neck, the way her curly dark hair caressed the side of her face with loving care.

It wasn't until she turned her head slightly toward him that his reverence halted and he realized that she was crying. His heart convulsed at the sight and he leaned out the window.

"Mary...Marina," he yelled, seeing her jump in surprise at the sound of his voice. "What's wrong?"

"Would you please stop peeping in on me," she exclaimed, her voice husky with emotion.

"Marina, talk to me. Why are you crying?" He stepped out onto the fire escape.

"I'm not crying," Marina protested, swiping angrily at her cheeks. "Dooley, please...just...just leave it alone."

But he couldn't just leave it alone. She was crying, and nobody should cry alone. For the second time since coming to New York City, Dooley found himself climbing down his fire escape and up hers. When he reached her window, he paused out on the platform, then climbed inside.

With a sigh of resignation, Marina dropped the letter at her side and got up off her sofa and faced him. "You are the most persistent man I've ever known," she said, gesturing for him to advance into the apartment.

"What's wrong?" he asked softly. He placed an arm around her shoulders and led her back over to the sofa where they both sat down.

For a long moment Marina didn't answer. She wasn't accustomed to sharing her feelings, had never been allowed the luxury of having somebody who cared to share them with. She felt as if she should resent Dooley's uninvited intrusion, but she didn't. Instead, she felt a certain strength in his presence. She handed him the letter she'd received that afternoon.

She watched as he scanned the short contents, his face reflecting his sympathy for her.

When he had finished reading, he set the letter aside and reached for her, pulling her into his arms and holding her close. "I'm sorry, Marina. It's always hard to lose somebody close to you."

Marina felt a stinging in her eyes and she burrowed her head in his shoulder.

"I assume this is the aunt who raised you?" he asked, gently stroking her back with a rhythm that was soothing.

She nodded her head, tears leaking out from beneath her tightly closed eyes. "You don't understand," she said, her voice muffled against the collar of his shirt. Suddenly, the tears were coming faster than she could swallow them, overwhelming the control she'd tried to maintain. She choked, the sobs surprising even her as her grief conquered her.

"That's it, cry it out," Dooley murmured, pulling her even closer against him, as if he could absorb her pain through physical closeness.

The feel of his arms so tightly surrounding her, the warmth of his closeness, the genuine caring she felt emanating from him, broke loose a dam of emotions that had been tightly reined for a very long time. Marina cried for the loss of her parents so long ago. She cried for the isolation and loneliness that had marked her youth. She cried tears that had been trapped inside her for so long, finding safety in Dooley's arms.

Dooley sensed that it was more than the death of her aunt that caused Marina to cry. Her sobs were too deep, too profound to come from this single moment. Yet he asked her no questions, he simply held her. And it was at that moment that Dooley realized that he was in love with Mary Ann Rayburn. The realization didn't surprise him. What did surprise him was how right it felt.

When she was finally finished sobbing, leaving behind only an occasional hiccup and a very wet spot on Dooley's shirt, she pulled away from him as if embarrassed by her display.

"I'm sorry," she said, self-consciously rubbing at her reddened eyes. "I can't imagine what made me break down like that."

"I'd say a cry like that was a long time coming," Dooley observed gently.

Marina reached for a tissue out of the box on the end table and finished swiping the last of her lingering tears.

"I'm sorry you lost your aunt. You must have been quite close."

Marina emitted a small laugh. "Actually, we weren't close at all." She picked up the letter from the sofa and stared at it for a long moment. "This was written by a neighbor who thought I would want to know that my aunt was buried a week ago." She set the letter down on the coffee table before them. "My uncle didn't think to let me know earlier, so that I might have attended the funeral."

"Maybe he was too distraught, not thinking properly," Dooley suggested.

Marina shook her head. "It's more than that. When I first read the letter, I sat here and waited for grief to overtake me, but there was nothing. I was just empty inside." She looked at him incredulously, her eyes a shade of midnight blue. "How do you grieve for somebody you never really knew?"

"What do you mean?"

Marina sighed, thinking back into her past, finding the memories achingly painful. She wrapped her arms around herself, as if seeking some comfort from within herself. "My aunt and uncle were good, hard-working people, but they had no idea what to do with a child. They chose not to have children, then my parents died and suddenly my aunt and uncle had to raise me. I was raised in silence, with no hugs, no physical demonstrations of love. They fed me, clothed me, provided the necessities of life, but they never knew me." She bit her bottom lip. "I grew up feeling invisible." There was a hollowness inside her, but surprisingly there was also a sense of relief. It was the first time she had talked about her past with anyone. Now she realized that talking about it had somehow robbed her memories of their pain-evoking intensity.

"You aren't invisible to me," Dooley said, his eyes emitting the emerald warmth that pulled at her, enticing her to melt into the heat they offered. He reached out and touched her cheek in a light caress.

Marina smiled up at him. "You're a nice man, Dooley James."

"I try to be." He returned her smile.

"I owe you an apology."

"For what?" His forehead wrinkled in curiosity.

"For the things I said to you last night."

Dooley smiled at her once again, his hand still lightly caressing her cheek. "My mother always told me not to pay much attention to words spoken in anger or fear."

"Your mother is a smart woman," Marina returned, closing her eyes, wanting...needing the heat his touch manufactured to ward off the cold chill that still suffused her body.

She leaned her head back as his hand continued to caress her cheek, then moved over to smooth the sensitive area of her throat.

Slowly, the heat of his fingertips began to flow inside her, forming a coil of heat that unfurled in her stomach and expanded.

She felt him move closer to her, his hip next to hers, his leg pressing inward against hers. Gone were the mental barriers she'd tried to erect, dissipated were the defenses that should have kept her maintaining distance.

Instead, there was only a need to be held. She felt achingly vulnerable, and she found herself wondering once again what magic it was that Dooley possessed.

He seemed so uncomplicated compared to the men she'd dated in the past. There would be no game playing with Dooley. He shot from the hip and damn the consequences. She caught her breath as his fingertip caress on her neck was replaced with his mouth. Slowly, sensually, he trailed a row of kisses down the column of her neck, his breath warm and sweet against her skin.

He placed the palms of his hands on either side of her face. "Marina...open your eyes and look at me."

She did as he bid her, flickering open her eyes and staring into his gaze. As he kissed her lips, her gaze remained locked with his, and in his eyes she saw warmth and caring, and beneath that the smoldering fire of desire.

For the first time in her life, she felt validated, certain that she wasn't invisible, that she did indeed matter. And she wanted the magic of the moment to last forever. She wanted to lose herself in this man with his country ways and homespun charm.

She turned slightly on the sofa, wrapping her arms around his neck to tangle in the soft copper-colored hair at his nape. Without thought, acting only on instinct, she pressed her body more fully against his. Her action caused him to moan inside her mouth, and with an easy, fluid movement, he eased her sideways so she was lying on the sofa, his body covering hers like the warmth of a favorite blanket.

She could feel his desire for her and all the fantasies she'd entertained about him exploded in her head, making her arch against him in an attempt to show him her acquiescence.

His eyes deepened to the color of ancient jade, and his hand traveled down the length of her neck, across her collarbone, down to gently caress the swell of her breast. There was a question in his eyes, and she answered it by reaching up to unbutton her blouse. She unfastened the first two buttons, then his hand moved hers and he took over the task. When he was finished, he brushed the blouse aside, baring her creamy skin and lacy bra.

Marina closed her eyes once again, giving herself to the languid heat his caresses evoked. He moved slowly, as if they had all the time of eternity, each stroke building on the base of passion that had been stirred.

When he deftly unsnapped the center fastening of her bra, and his hands covered the swell of her bare breasts, Marina knew there was no turning back, nor did she want to. This felt good…right. She wanted to be here in Dooley's arms, experiencing the fever of Dooley's lovemaking.

Dooley was a lost man, lost in the intensity of his emotions where Marina was concerned. He wanted to touch every inch of her, taste the sweetness of her heated flesh. He dipped his head and touched his tongue to the pink tip of her breast, feeling the way it leapt eagerly at his touch. She moaned deep in her throat, one that pulled an answering moan from him. She was so beautiful.

His hands trembled as he hurriedly unbuttoned his shirt and pulled it off, wanting to feel her bare breasts against the heat of his own skin. Her hands danced across his back, lingering on the hard muscles, the sharply etched planes of his broadness. Unconsciously his hips moved against hers, finding a rhythm that was easy, provocative, making her gasp with pleasure.

There was a pounding in Marina's ears, a loud thudding that made thought impossible. It wasn't until Dooley shifted off her that she realized the pounding was coming from her door.

"Don't answer it," Dooley whispered.

Marina nodded, too dazed to speak, wanting only to continue what they had begun. But the knocking intensified.

"Marina...it's me and Susan." Robert's voice drifted through the locked door.

Marina sat up, quickly re-clasping her bra. "I forgot, I'm baby-sitting tonight...."

Dooley grabbed his shirt off the floor, knowing the spell was broken, the moment was lost.

"Just a minute, Robert," Marina yelled, buttoning her blouse and smoothing a hand through her tousled hair. She looked at Dooley with regret. "I'm sorry," she said softly.

He shrugged, his green eyes gleaming with an unnatural brightness. "There will be other times," he said, his voice holding unspoken promises.

No, there won't, Marina thought as she went to open the door. What had just transpired between them had been a mistake, an unguarded moment that she'd see would never happen again. Making love with

Dooley would be a devastating mistake. She had the feeling that making love with him would mark her forever, would be an experience she would never, ever be able to forget.

Her body still tingled from the sensations he'd stirred, and she couldn't let it happen again. She had to be strong... strong enough to fight the overpowering forces that existed between the two of them.

"Hi, kids," she greeted the two who came through the door. The two returned her greeting as they came into the apartment.

"Are you gonna tell us more mouse stories?" Susan asked as she smiled shyly at Dooley, who was still seated on the sofa.

"Maybe later," Marina answered, watching as Robert eyed Dooley suspiciously.

"What are you doing here?" the little boy asked the big man.

"I was just visiting Marina," Dooley said, his gaze on her so warm it brought a blush to her cheeks.

Robert looked first at Dooley, then at Marina. "Were you guys kissing and stuff?"

"Robert, what would make you think that?" Marina asked self-consciously, her blush deepening.

"'Cause your face is all red like Mom's was the other night when I got up for a drink of water and caught her and Gregory kissing." Robert flopped down onto the sofa next to Dooley. "So, were you kissing Marina?"

"Robert, I never tell my secrets to eight-year-old boys," Dooley exclaimed. "Come see me when you're a little older and I'll tell you all about kissing."

"I think kissing is yucky," Susan announced, reaching for the basket of Marina's mice. She got down on the floor and pulled out several little creatures, immediately becoming engrossed in a world inhabited only by them.

Robert got up to go to the bathroom. When he'd disappeared, Dooley looked at Marina, regret shining from his eyes. "I feel like I need to run around a football field to release some tension."

Once again Marina felt a warm flush covering her cheeks, knowing instantly what kind of tension he was referring to. "Maybe you should try a cold shower," she suggested.

"I'd have to stand beneath the spray of a fire hydrant to relieve this amount of pressure," he said with a wide grin. "Actually, I think there's only one cure for me, and I guess that's out of the question, at least for tonight."

Forever, Marina thought, her gaze not meeting his. She decided to pop some popcorn, wanting something to do, something to concentrate on besides Dooley. She now wished he'd just go back to his own apartment, leave her alone to get her tumultuous emotions firmly under control. As she got out the saucepan and oil, she glanced back at Dooley, who was now sitting on the floor next to Susan, talking to her in low tones.

Dooley James . . . how had she been so foolish to allow him to creep into her life, into her heart? For that's where he was now, firmly entrenched, and she wondered when he finally returned to South Carolina how much time would have to pass before she would forget him.

Thank God the kids had arrived and stopped her before she made a mistake that wouldn't easily be rectified. She poured the popcorn into the hot oil and covered the pan.

She had to concentrate on what she wanted out of life, and it positively did not include a life in South Carolina on a plantation with Dooley. New York City was where she belonged, pursuing her childhood dreams. What frightened her was that with each day that passed, with every moment she spent with Dooley, her dreams of stardom seemed more distant, less important.

As the first kernel popped, Marina suddenly realized exactly what was happening. She was falling in love with Dooley James. The kernels exploded in the pan, and Marina's thoughts did the same in her head. Dear God, how had this happened? What was she going to do about it? How could fate be so cruel as to make her choose between love and her dreams? For surely that's what would eventually have to happen. If she continued a relationship with Dooley, eventually she would have to make a choice and no matter what choice was made, she would lose.

The popcorn finished popping and she poured it into a bowl, realizing she was on the verge of a mammoth headache. It was then she realized Robert was still in the bathroom.

She set the bowl of popcorn on the coffee table and knocked on the bathroom door. "Robert, is everything all right in there?"

"Sure," he answered, then giggled. "But I'm not coming out."

Marina frowned. "What do you mean, you aren't coming out?"

"I'm gonna stay in here all night until my mom gets home."

Dooley, hearing what was transpiring, stood up and joined Marina at the door. "Robert, you don't want to stay in the bathroom all night. Why don't you come on out of there."

"No. I don't want to." Robert's voice held the stubbornness that only an eight-year-old could generate.

"Robert, this isn't funny. You need to come out of there right now." Dooley put as much sternness in his voice as possible, but he was met with a giggle, then silence. Marina and Dooley looked at each other, unsure of what to do. "Robert, if I have to break down the door, I'm going to be very angry," Dooley warned.

"Go ahead and break down the door," Robert replied.

"Gregory says Robert does stuff like this for attention," Susan exclaimed.

"Gregory is probably right," Dooley replied thoughtfully. "Why don't the three of us sit down and eat some popcorn. You can tell Susan one of your mice stories," he suggested.

"But what about Robert?" Marina frowned worriedly.

Dooley took Marina by the arm and led her over to the sofa. "Let's just ignore him and see what happens."

Marina looked at him dubiously, not wanting anything to happen to Robert. Finally she nodded and looked at Susan.

"Susan, you want to hear a mouse story?" Marina asked, motioning the little girl to crawl up onto her lap.

"Oh, yes, you tell me good stories," she exclaimed eagerly, getting up in Marina's lap and sticking a thumb in her mouth.

"Once upon a time, there was a mouse without a house..." At first, as Marina began her story, she was acutely conscious of Dooley's presence. She could feel the heat of his gaze, almost taste the remembered sweetness of his lips, but as the words flowed out of her, she lost herself in the pleasure of her storytelling. There was nothing more wonderful than sitting and telling her stories, breathing the sweet scent of Susan's hair, feeling the wiggly warmth of the child on her lap.

Dooley watched her, loving her with his eyes. She was so beautiful and she looked content ... right with the child on her lap, telling the whimsical stories that had sustained her through her lonely youth.

Within minutes, Robert peeked his head out of the bathroom door, unable to resist the lure of the story. Several seconds later, he joined them on the sofa, instantly becoming engrossed in Marina's tale.

The picture they made was that of a family, and Dooley felt the ache that had been inside him for so long subside. This was what he wanted from life, his own family. He wanted children, and a woman who could tell them nighttime stories of charming creatures. He wanted Marina. He loved her. Now all he had to do was somehow convince her that she wanted the same thing.

Chapter Eight

"Marina, darling, you aren't concentrating," Holiday Maxwell, Marina's drama teacher chided her.

"I'm sorry. I guess I have a lot of things on my mind today," Marina replied, sitting down onto the jungle-print sofa in Holiday's living room.

"That's not good enough." Holiday joined her on the sofa, her bracelets jingling musically as she swept a hand through her vivid red hair. "I've told you from the very beginning that acting is more than a job and will demand more of you than anything else you can pursue. You can't have other things on your mind. It demands total concentration, complete commitment." She paused a moment to pet the large Persian cat that hopped up into her lap. "Now, shall we try it again?"

Marina nodded and began the scene again, but as before, she knew it wasn't working. She just couldn't seem to concentrate on the words she was saying. "It's just not right. I guess I'm just not good today." She stood up, deciding that nothing more could be accomplished while her head was so full of conflicting emotions.

Holiday nodded and stood up, the cat meowing his complaint. "That's what I'm talking about, dear. There is no such thing as 'not today,' or 'I have too much on my mind.' In this business the audience demands your all, and they'll know if you cheat." Holiday smiled, the enigmatic one that had thrilled audiences of the big screen for years in the 1950s. "Well, I guess I've given you enough of a lecture for today." She leaned down and scooped up the fat, pampered cat. "Poopsie here gets upset when I lecture." She stroked the cat's thick fur lovingly, then looked back at Marina. "Go and think about our little chat. I'll see you next week."

Think... Marina shook her head as she left Holiday's brownstone. It seemed that all she'd been doing for the past twenty-four hours was thinking. And the only thing all that mental exercise had managed to do was make her more confused than ever.

She looked at her wristwatch, realizing she only had a half hour before she had to be at the theater for her first official rehearsal. There wouldn't be time for lunch. "Get used to it, kid. This is the life you want," she muttered. *Isn't it?* a little voice inside added.

"Shut up," she hissed to the inner intrusion, making a passing pedestrian stare at her warily.

She grinned, realizing she couldn't mutter to herself without people thinking she was crazy. "But what's one more loony tune on the streets of New York?" she said aloud with a laugh.

As she walked to the subway that would take her to the theater, she thought back over the previous night.

Dooley had stayed until she'd finished telling the kids several mouse stories, then he had told them good-night and had gone back to his own apartment.

Even after he was gone and the kids had fallen asleep, she'd felt his presence lingering. The woodsy scent of him remained in the air, and the remembered feel of his arms surrounding her still burned her skin.

After Josie picked up the children, before Marina went to sleep, she turned off all her lights and sat at her window, staring at the one across the alleyway. She could almost feel the warmth flowing from his window to hers, not the heat of the summer night, not a physical sensation at all. Rather it was an emotional heat that bathed her soul, seeking out the areas of darkness and filling them with light.

She'd never before felt the way she had when she'd been lying in his arms. Somehow he'd managed to banish the darkness of her youth, make her feel whole and sane.

Surely it was simply a matter of him coming along when she was particularly vulnerable. The letter telling of her aunt's death had brought to the surface wounds that had never healed, needs that had never been fulfilled. It had simply been a matter of timing and circumstances that had made her respond to him so eagerly, so hungrily.

She probably would have responded the same way to anyone who'd offered her kindness under the circumstances. This thought was comforting, but it ran untrue.

I can't fall in love with Dooley, she told herself as she fed in her token and passed through the turnstile, then walked onto the subway platform. *I'm a city mouse and he's a country mouse. He won't even get on a subway, for goodness' sake. He could never remain here in this city and I refuse to leave here. This is where I belong, on the stage in front of thousands of people. I absolutely refuse to be in love with Dooley James,* she thought with determination. But she had a feeling that although her head was listening, her heart had gone deaf.

It was nearly dusk as Marina dragged herself home. The rehearsal that was to have lasted three hours had run nearly double that and she was completely wrung out.

The rehearsal had not been a particularly pleasant experience. Although it had been just a read-through, within the first few minutes it had been obvious that the leading man and leading woman shared a past, and abhorred each other. They'd spent the entire time hissing insults to each other beneath their breaths, making the air tense and unpleasant for everyone else.

The director was a balding, cigar chain-smoker who called all women "babe," and the men "dude." He had a raspy voice that grated and he seemed to like the sound of it, for he droned on interminably.

On the whole, it had been an unsettling day, nothing like what Marina had always imagined. There had been no glamour, no feeling of specialness.

What did you expect? she chided herself, unlocking her apartment door and flopping down tiredly onto the sofa. It was a first rehearsal. Of course there was no magic, no glamour. That would come later, on opening night when she finally heard the music of a roomful of people applauding.

I'm just tired, she thought, rationalizing away the disappointment of the rehearsal. "Tired and hungry," she said aloud as her stomach grumbled its complaint.

She'd just finished cooking a TV dinner when a knock fell on her door. She opened it to see Cynthia, her waitress friend from the restaurant.

"Cynthia, what are you doing here?" Marina ushered her friend inside, surprised and pleased by the unexpected visit.

"I stopped by the restaurant tonight to pick up my check and Nick told me you got a part in a play." She flopped down onto the sofa and looked at Marina expectantly. "So... tell me all about it."

Marina laughed self-consciously. "It's not that big a deal. You know the Trinity Theater? That's where the play will be and it's a funny murder mystery with romantic overtones. I play the leading man's sister. I only have about ten lines."

"You've got a speaking role? Oh, I'm so jealous!" Cynthia patted the sofa next to her. "Well, sit down here and tell me more about it."

Marina did just that. As she told Cynthia the plot of the play and described her role, she found her enthusiasm returning, fed by Cynthia's excitement and envy.

"Well, girl, it sounds like your run of bad luck has been broken. You're finally on your way," Cynthia observed when Marina had finished.

Yes, but is it the direction I really want to go in? a small voice whispered in the back of Marina's head. She consciously ignored it, refusing to consider the doubts it chattered. *Stuff a sock in it,* she told the inner voice.

"Hey, what's this?" Cynthia asked, spying Marina's sewing basket near her feet. She reached down and grabbed one of the stuffed mice, her face wreathing into a grin of delight. "Did you make this?" she asked curiously.

Marina nodded, a flush of pleasure sweeping through her as she saw Cynthia's expression of awe.

"Gosh, Marina, this is terrific." Cynthia ran her fingertips over the mouse's delicate features, down over the little pink tu-tu that made the mouse a balle-

rina. "It makes you smile just to look at it," Cynthia
exclaimed.

"They're just something I mess around with in my
spare time," Marina replied.

"I wish I had talent like this." Cynthia set the little
creature back in the basket, then stood up. "I'd better get out of here. I've got a date in less than an
hour."

After Cynthia left, Marina went back to the sofa
and sat down, reaching for her sewing basket.

Talent... She'd never thought of her little mouse
friends as products of her own talent. To her, the
whimsical creatures had always been a means to an
end, providing the finances needed to carry her from
Arkansas to New York City. But she had been in New
York City for over a year and still she continued making the mice, finding joy in giving the creatures as
gifts, pleasure in the mere act of creating new and different ones.

She stared at the mouse in her hand, suddenly remembering Dooley's business proposition at the restaurant on the day they'd gone sight-seeing. Sell her
mice in his restaurants? On the day he'd made the
suggestion, she'd dismissed it from her mind, afraid
that in deciding to sell the mice, she would somehow
return to the unhappiness of her past.

Now, when she reached inside and searched her
soul, she found that the baggage of her past, which she
had subconsciously carried around for so long, was
gone. Sure, there was still sadness at the lost years, a

mourning for the people who had raised her but whom she had never known. However, the aching loneliness, the painful isolation was gone, purged by the tears she'd shed in the strength of Dooley's arms.

She'd begun making the mice long ago to feed her loneliness, and while they no longer served that particular purpose, she suddenly realized they still did provide an immense amount of pleasure.

Sell the mice in Dooley's restaurants... she mused, *where lots of children would have access to them.* She had probably close to twenty made, packed in a box in the closet. She could at least give those to Dooley, have him put them in the restaurants and see if they really would sell.

Decision made, she got up off the sofa and crossed to the window. Leaning out, she called across the alley. "Dooley? Are you in there?" She waited a moment, then called once again, this time a little louder.

She was surprised at the pleasure that swept over her when he stuck his head out the window and grinned at her, his face illuminated by a nearby streetlight.

"Were you serious the other day about selling my mice in your restaurants?"

"Absolutely," he answered without hesitation. "I think it's a terrific idea. They'd sell faster than you could make them. Do you want me to come over there so we can talk about it?"

Marina hesitated, noticing the distinct eagerness in his tone. If he were to come over, there would be no baby-sitting charges to interrupt should things get out of control. Dooley James after dark was definitely dangerous and Marina wasn't willing to chance another physical encounter until she knew exactly where her emotions were where he was concerned.

"No, we can talk in the morning," she finally answered.

"That's a terrific idea," their grouchy downstairs "friend" yelled.

Marina smiled and waved to Dooley, then she moved away from the window, letting him know the conversation was at an end.

She felt renewed, invigorated by her decision to sell her mice. She was also exhausted by the long day. She pulled her blinds tightly closed, changed into a nightshirt and made up her bed on the sofa. Once she'd turned out the lights, she reached up and reopened the shades, hoping for a stirring of air to relieve the heat.

All the weather forecasters were predicting an unseasonably early heat wave, and Marina dreaded the coming of the hot days. In no place else on earth was summer quite so cruel as in New York City. The city of concrete and steel retained the heat, magnifying stench, firing tempers, raising the incidence of crimes.

Summer in South Carolina is probably quite different, Marina thought, stifling a yawn with the back of her hand. In South Carolina there would probably be night breezes, filled with the fragrance of sun-warmed grass and wildflowers. The breeze would rustle the leaves of the trees, make the needles of the pines whisper a song of sweet dreams.

She punched her pillow and turned over, irritated by the sounds of the traffic, the distant wail of a siren, somebody yelling down the hallway. Had it always been so darned noisy? She couldn't remember the city sounds bothering her as much as they were at this moment. *I'm just overtired,* she thought. She punched her pillow once again and squeezed her eyes tightly closed, willing sleep to overtake her quickly.

"Marina...wait up." Marina slowed her fast pace down the sidewalk and turned to see Dooley running after her. As always, his open smile and genuine pleasure at seeing her made her smile in return, despite the fact that her eyes felt gritty from lack of sleep. "I thought we were going to get together and talk about your mice this morning," he said, falling into step beside her.

"I intended for us to, but Nick called me from the restaurant and asked me to work an early shift," she explained. "He's been so nice about changing my hours because of play rehearsals, I didn't feel like I could turn him down. We'll have to postpone our talk until later."

"You look tired," Dooley observed, his gaze as warm as a caress across her cheek.

"I am," she admitted. "I had trouble sleeping last night. I was overtired, and the heat bothered me."

They walked a few steps in silence, then Dooley took a deep breath. "This is the best time of the day in this city. It's early enough that the crazies are all still sleeping, and the smog hasn't completely settled in yet."

"Maybe New York is growing on you," Marina replied, surprised at the flare of hope that appeared inside her. Maybe she'd misjudged him. Maybe he really could adapt to life in the big city. "If you stayed here long enough, you'd probably become a happy, well-adjusted urbanite like the rest of us."

Dooley shook his head, his hair sparking as if kissed by a god of fire. "No way." His forehead wrinkled thoughtfully. "I think if I had to stay here for too long, I'd start to die. Just a little bit, day by day, I'd crumble from homesickness, pining for the fields and mountains back home. I'm a country man through and through, and I don't think that's something that can be changed."

The flare of hope in her was doused like a flame beneath water. He would die if he had to remain in the city, and she would die if she was stuck someplace out in the country without a theater, without an audience.

Fate had been cruel to bring Dooley into her life, then give them both directions that would forever keep them apart or destroy one of them.

"Have you had any luck locating a site for your restaurant yet?" she asked, changing the subject.

"Not yet. My real-estate agent has accused me of being difficult to please."

"Are you?" She looked up at him curiously.

"About my restaurants, I guess I am," he confessed. "But I have certain standards I won't compromise."

"Well, I guess I'll see you later," she said as they came to the door of the restaurant.

Dooley reached out and swiped a strand of her hair from her face, his touch so achingly tender that Marina once again felt a flare of specialness coursing through her. "Try to get some rest sometime today," he said softly, his fingertips lingering on the soft curve of her cheek.

She nodded and whirled into the restaurant, escaping from the caring she saw in his eyes, the crazy emotions he always managed to make her feel.

Oh, yes, fate had been cruel to bring Dooley into her life. But she would see to it that fate didn't have the last laugh. She was on a course set for success, and she wasn't going to allow her own weakness where Dooley was concerned to become an obstacle that threw her off course.

"Hey, doll, I'm so glad you're here," Nick said, approaching Marina hurriedly. "We've got a party of twenty coming in for breakfast in about fifteen minutes, and the tables aren't even set up yet. Susan called in suffering from morning sickness and I'm going a little crazy."

"Don't worry, I'll get right to it," she replied, grateful for anything that would take her mind off the russet-haired country man.

She didn't think about Dooley again until she was serving the party of twenty. The group was real-estate agents from various Manhattan offices. As she served them their breakfast platters, she overheard a couple of them talking about a restaurant that had just come on the market.

"Fantastic location . . . a lot of pass-by traffic," a sophisticated-looking blonde was telling her table-mates. "The restaurant was doing quite well, but the owner recently lost his wife and wants to move out to California where the rest of his family is located."

"You certainly won't have trouble moving it, not at that reasonable asking price," observed another of the ladies at the table.

"Excuse me, I couldn't help overhearing your conversation," Marina said to the blonde. "I've got a friend who's looking for a place to open a restaurant. This sounds like something he might be interested in."

"Great, let me give you my card." The blonde fumbled in her purse and withdrew a gold-embossed business card.

Business must be thriving in Manhattan, Marina thought as she looked at the card. "Krista Hoffman," she read the name.

"That's me," the woman said with a smile. "Tell your friend to give me a call and I'll see what I can do for him."

Marina nodded, stuck the card in her pocket, then returned to work. The rest of the morning flew by, and it wasn't until later that afternoon as she walked home from work that she withdrew the business card from her pocket and looked at it once again. She would stop by Dooley's apartment and give it to him.

As she walked, a sudden thought crossed her mind. If she gave Dooley the card and the restaurant was exactly what he was looking for, she would expedite the process that would take him back to South Carolina.

Isn't that what you want? she asked herself, unsurprised when there was no easy answer. Yes, a part of her wanted Dooley gone, and another part wished she had never met him, that he'd never entered her life and become a part of her world.

She gripped the business card more firmly in her hand and walked with determined footsteps to his apartment. If he went home now, she could handle it. She would miss him, always wonder what might have been, but the feelings she had for him were in infancy stages and if not nurtured, if ignored, they would eventually pass.

She got to the door of his apartment and knocked loudly, then waited. There was no answer. She rapped a second time and still there was no reply. He wasn't in. She slipped the card back into her pocket and turned and left. She'd have to catch up with him later. Besides, she did want to talk to him about her mice. She could give him the business card at that time.

As she went into her own apartment building, she encountered Gregory waiting for the elevator.

"Don't you look nice," she observed, noting the suit that made her friend look more like a banker than an actor. There was a touch of sadness in her as she realized she hadn't seen him for the past couple of days. Already their close friendship was pulling apart due to their differences in career choices.

"I've been job hunting," Gregory said as they waited for the elevator.

"I thought you were talking with Dooley about working for him in one of his restaurants."

"I was ... I still am, but I'm also looking around to see what other positions are available," he explained.

"How's Josie?" she asked with a sly grin.

"She's the most frustrating woman I've ever met. Did you know she eats mayo-and-pickle sandwiches for breakfast?" He shivered with revulsion.

"Oh, are you at the breakfast-together stage?"

Gregory blushed slightly, making Marina laugh.

"Saved by the bell," Gregory said as the elevator pinged its arrival and the doors slid open.

"You don't know where Dooley is right now, do you?" Marina asked as Gregory held the doors open for her.

"Sure, he took Robert and Susan down to the little park area in the next block."

"What's he doing taking Robert and Susan to a park?" she asked curiously, hesitating before entering the elevator.

Gregory shrugged. "He's being a good Samaritan. He knows I'm job hunting and Josie is working, so for the past couple of days he's been taking the time to take the kids to the park." Gregory grinned. "Dooley

seems to think it isn't fitting for the kids to be confined in an apartment. They need the feel of grass beneath their feet.'' He stepped into the elevator and
looked at her expectantly. "Are you coming?"

"No, I think I'll walk down and find Dooley. I've
got some information about a restaurant for sale that
might interest him.'' She waved as the elevator doors
closed, making Gregory disappear from sight.

How like Dooley to try to give a couple of city-
dwelling kids a little bit of the country. She smiled. She
had a feeling if Dooley had his way, there would be no
big cities, no urban areas. Her smile slowly faded as
she once again realized the enormous conflict that
would forever make it impossible for a relationship
with him.

She needed more than he could ever offer, and he
couldn't be different than what he was. He'd made it
very clear to her that he couldn't be happy here in the
city.

It took her only a few minutes to find the park
Gregory had spoken of. It really wasn't much of a
park, just a lot that boasted a single huge tree, patchy
areas of grass, a few wooden benches, a couple of
seesaws, a swing set and a slide.

Although the area was small, there were several
groups of children playing, watched by the adults who
sat on the benches, seeking relief from the heat in the
shade of the tree.

Despite the fact that the park buzzed with activity,
Marina spied Dooley immediately. He stood at the

foot of the big slide, looking magnificent in a T-shirt and a pair of shorts that exposed firm, masculine legs covered with red-gold hair. The sun played on his head, like an impish fire spirit enjoying the unruliness of the copper strands. Marina was amused to see that he was barefoot.

How had a country man like this managed to put together such a thriving business as six restaurants? She had a feeling his success came solely from his love of life, his enthusiasm that was contagious to everyone around him. He was probably adored by his employees.

Marina watched the scene before her. Susan sat at the top of the slide, her hands tightly grasping the railing that kept her from descending down. "You promise you'll catch me, Uncle Dooley?" she asked.

Uncle Dooley? How easily Dooley had been accepted into the lives of Robert and Susan. How many broken hearts he would leave behind when he finally returned to South Carolina.

"Come on, Squirt. I promise I'll catch you," Dooley yelled back to the child. As Marina watched, Susan released her hands and slid down the slide, squealing with delight as she reached the bottom and Dooley picked her up and swung her around. Her childish giggles mingled with Dooley's deep, pleasant laughter, creating a strange buzzing sound in Marina's ears. As Susan reached her arms around Dooley's neck and planted a kiss on his cheek, Marina thought of how right the big man looked with a child.

It was easy to imagine him with a child of his own. No child of Dooley's would ever want for love and affection.

She twirled around, suddenly needing to be away from the scene that whispered with promises, pulled at her emotions.

She stumbled down the street toward her apartment, trembling with the swelling realization that was pounding inside her. She'd thought her love for Dooley was in its infancy stages, that it wasn't too late to turn back. But in that single moment of seeing him and Susan together, Marina's love for the big country man had blossomed into full fruition.

All the dreams she'd had for herself, all the years of planning and working to make it in New York, to hear the sound of hundreds applauding her, teetered, weighed on the other end by Dooley. Up and down went the seesaw in her head, taunting her, tormenting her with visions of a life on the stage, and a life with Dooley.

It had been her desire and ambition that had seen her through the lonely years of her youth. She couldn't relinquish her dreams. She wanted the approval of hundreds, she wanted the love that emanated from an audience. Dooley's love would never be enough, would it?

When the seesaw finally stopped, her career was on firm ground, and Dooley was flailing in the air. Her decision was made. Dooley was dangerous. She recognized that she loved him, and she was making a conscious decision to turn her back on that love. It was called survival, and she now knew that Dooley had to be avoided at all costs.

Chapter Nine

Dooley whistled a cheerful melody as he got off the elevator and headed for Marina's apartment door.

It had been three days since he'd seen her, and he was surprised by how much he hungered to be in her company, how much he needed to see her lovely face, the smile that made him ache inside with want.

Oh, you've got it bad, he thought. And the problem was, he wasn't sure how Marina felt about him. Oh, sure, he'd tasted desire on her lips when he'd kissed her, felt her body respond with a wild hunger that had fed his own. Physical attraction was one thing... the kind of soul connection he wanted was something else again.

He'd been elated the other night when she'd yelled across the alleyway that she was willing to sell her mice in the restaurants. As a businessman, he knew it would be a successful venture. But, more than that, he'd seen it as a concession, a step forward, a decision that brought their life-styles closer together.

But she hadn't followed through on it. He'd waited the past three days for her to come by, contact him, talk about this new business deal. She hadn't. Didn't she know how talented she was? Not only in making the mice, but in telling the stories she told Robert and Susan. She was a talented storyteller, and it was easy to imagine her telling their children her delightful tales.

He'd gotten up this morning and decided it was time to take matters into his own hands. Time was running out, and he needed to know if there was a chance for him and Marina. He loved her as he had never loved anyone before in his life. He wanted with her the same sort of things his brothers had found with their wives. He needed to know if he was going to leave New York City with a broken heart.

He reached her door and raised his hand to knock. Before his knuckles could connect with the wood, the door flew open and Marina squealed in surprise.

"Jeez, Dooley, you almost gave me a heart attack." She stepped out of the door and pulled it closed behind her.

"Marina, we need to talk," he said without preamble.

Her face flushed and her eyes didn't quite meet his. "Dooley, I was just on my way to rehearsal. I really don't have time to talk right now. Maybe another time.''

There was a distance in her voice that had never been there before, a distance that made Dooley look at her intently, wondering what had caused it. There was no hint of Mary Ann in her persona this morning. Her makeup was carefully applied, hiding the freckles he loved. She looked sophisticated and professional, but Dooley refused to be put off by her appearance. As she started down the hallway toward the elevator, he followed behind her.

"Marina...is something wrong? Have I done something to upset you?''

"Of course not.'' She laughed, but it sounded forced to Dooley. She pushed the elevator button, looking grateful when the doors immediately opened. She stepped inside and he quickly followed.

"Then why do I get the feeling that you've been avoiding me the last couple of days?''

"Don't be ridiculous,'' she returned, still not looking at him. "Why on earth would I be avoiding you?''

"That's what I'm trying to figure out.''

She ran a hand through her hair, a gesture that made her curls ripple across her shoulders. Dooley balled his hands into fists, fighting the impulse to reach out and tangle himself in its thick richness. "I'm just tremendously busy,'' she explained, moving out of the elevator the minute the doors slid open. "I've been working mornings at the restaurant and trying to fit in extra drama lessons with Holiday, my drama coach. They've moved up the opening for the play...money problems or something. So we're doubling up rehearsals to be ready for opening night in two weeks."

"Isn't that unusual?" Dooley asked curiously, following her out into the brilliant sunshine.

She shrugged her shoulders. "In this business, nothing is unusual."

"You never got back to me about selling your mice."

"I've changed my mind," she replied airily. "My career is time-consuming. I don't have time to put my energies into any other area."

There seemed to be a not-so-subtle warning in her words, and Dooley felt his heart thud painfully in his chest. But he'd never been a man to give up easily, especially when he believed the end result was well worth the effort.

"I found a location for the restaurant," he said.

"That's wonderful," she replied. "I guess that means you'll be leaving our fair city pretty soon."

Dooley reached out and grabbed her arm, causing her to stop the fast pace she'd been keeping. "Marina...we really need to talk."

She jerked her arm out of his grasp and continued walking. "We have nothing to talk about," she returned, her voice sounding determined and firm. When she reached the steps that led down to the subway station, she turned and looked at him. "Just leave it alone, Dooley,'' she said softly, then turned and ran down the stairs.

He stood for a moment, staring after her. Fear, that was what had been in her eyes. And in her fear, he felt a surge of hope. If she was frightened, then he must be a threat to everything she wanted, and if he was a threat it was because she cared for him more than she was admitting.

Taking a deep breath, he hurried after her, down into the dank dimness of the subterranean cave. Immediately he felt his heartbeat accelerate and a sick cramping begin in the pit of his stomach. He fought his need to turn and run back up into the sunlight, and instead kept his gaze focused on Marina, who was like a beacon of light leading him on.

He didn't have a token, so after only a moment's hesitation, he jumped over the turnstile and hurried toward Marina, who was stepping onto the train that had just pulled in.

Dooley stepped onto the train just as the doors slid closed, and with a whoosh and a squeal, the train began to move. The ride was fast, but certainly not smooth. The train jerked and swayed spasmodically, and the interior lights flickered on and off in an unpredictable rhythm. Still, Dooley made his way through the other passengers, focused only on the woman he loved, who was standing with her back to him, her hand grasping a handle overhead.

''Marina . . .'' He touched her back.

She turned and her eyes widened in shocked surprise. "Dooley, what are you doing here?"

All the things he'd wanted to say to her were trapped inside him. He couldn't tell her he loved her now, not in the middle of this crowd. He couldn't speak to her of future dreams and hopes when his heart was racing and sweat beaded up on his forehead. God, he needed to get off this train, out of this underground nightmare.

"Dooley, are you all right?" She laid a hand on his arm, looking at him with concern.

He shook his head, focusing on the blue depths of her eyes. "Mary Ann...I mean Marina...have dinner with me this Friday night."

Immediately she shook her head. "I can't. I've got a rehearsal."

Dooley took her hand. "Marina, please. It may be the last time we get together before I go home. We can eat after your rehearsal. Just a simple dinner...."

"Okay," she relented, stumbling slightly as the train slowed and lurched into the next station.

"Great," Dooley replied, then he turned around.

"Dooley, where are you going?"

He flashed her a sick smile. "I've got to get out of here." As the train came to a thundering halt, Dooley disappeared out the door.

Marina stared after him, unable to believe that he had braved his personal demons to get on the train and invite her to have dinner with him. *The man is crazy...and I must be even crazier to agree to eat with him,* she added thoughtfully.

Still, if he had found a site for his restaurant, then his business here was basically completed and he would soon be returning home. This thought should bring with it an enormous sense of relief. Dooley was the one temptation in her life, the one thing that made her ambition waver, made her feel less focused, less determined, more uncertain.

Yes, it should be an enormous relief that he would soon be gone and she would no longer feel so splintered. But instead of relief, she was surprised to feel despair.

This is a big mistake, Marina thought as she took the train home Friday night and thought of the dinner she would share with Dooley in the next hour.

Dooley...thoughts of the man had intruded at the strangest times through the past couple of days. She hadn't seen him since he'd walked out of the subway train, but that hadn't stopped thoughts of him from surfacing. She'd be in the wings of the stage at the theater, waiting for her cue, and suddenly Dooley would be there with her, his fresh, woodsy scent surrounding her, his face a picture etched in her mind. Or she'd be serving at the restaurant, and suddenly in a leafy salad or a sprig of parsley, she'd envision his green gaze, so warm and inviting, beckoning her to forget her dreams and fall into the passion, the desire he offered. It was distracting and irritating. He was a force in her life that she didn't want.

Things were going well at the theater. The actors had all learned their lines, the play was blocked and costumes were being readied. Rehearsals had intensified with opening night exactly a week away. There were whispers of financial problems, but Marina paid no attention. This was her first professional production, the first time she'd been on a stage since high school, and she was taking it one day at a time, savoring every sensation that came with the knowledge that finally she was doing what she'd always dreamed of doing. She anticipated next week, standing on the stage and for the first time hearing the sound of applause, knowing the audience accepted her, loved her.

Acceptance…love…that was what it was all about, feeding that part of her soul that had been undernourished as a child. There would be heartbreaks along the way, sacrifices to be made. Dooley was the first.

She reached her apartment and hurried inside, wanting to shower off the grime of the day before she went across the alleyway to Dooley's apartment. Besides, she was hoping a shower would give her a second wind. The rehearsal had been long and grueling and she was tired.

After showering, she dressed in a feminine, cool sundress, then stared thoughtfully at her reflection in the bathroom mirror. She considered putting on makeup, but knew the heat of the night would only melt it off. Instead she spritzed herself with her favorite perfume and pulled her hair up into a loose ponytail.

Tonight is my swan song where Dooley James is concerned, she told her reflection in the mirror. *He'll be gone soon and tonight will be the last time I'll be with him.* Certain of her inner strength, convinced of her commitment to her career, she left her apartment and headed for the apartment across the alleyway.

Dooley opened the door at the sound of her first knock. His green eyes swept over her appreciatively, making her wish she had chosen a gunnysack to wear rather than the sundress with the spaghetti straps that bared her shoulders to his heated gaze. "I'm glad you're here," he said as a greeting, making a wave of warmth sweep over her.

This is not only a big mistake, this is a major mistake, Marina thought as she stepped into the dimly lit apartment. The mood was set for romance. The small kitchen table was set beautifully with candles providing soft illumination. Music played from the stereo system, filling the room with an instrumental rendition of seduction.

"Make yourself at home. Dinner will be ready in just a few minutes," he instructed, going back over to the stove and stirring a pot of pasta.

Marina sat down on the sofa, her gaze lingering on him. He looked fantastic in a pair of white linen slacks and a sports shirt in a mint green that brought out the color of his eyes.

I've got to be strong, she reminded herself. She wished he were a backwoods hick with missing teeth and greasy hair.

This is a goodbye dinner, she reminded herself. *I have no place in his life and he has no place in mine. Country mouse and city mouse... there was no future for her with Dooley.*

"How was rehearsal tonight?" he asked, draining the pasta in the sink.

"Fantastic," she replied. "Even though we've squeezed six weeks of rehearsals into three, we're right where we need to be. Everything is coming along wonderfully. Opening night is just a week away and everyone is really excited." She stopped, realizing she was rambling. In an attempt to convince him, or herself? "Tell me about your restaurant," she asked.

He continued his dinner preparations as he spoke. "The agent found it for me. It's a terrific deal in a great location. The place just needs a little renovation work. I figure we'll be opening in about three months' time."

"So that means you'll be here in New York City for the next three months?" she asked, feeling a curious mixture of elation and fear at the thought.

"Oh, no, I've already talked with the construction people who will be doing the renovations. My business manager is flying in this week and he'll take over the day-to-day overseeing. It's time for me to return home. In fact, I made my plane reservations for next

Friday. I'm catching the red-eye.'' He placed several bowls on the table, then smiled at her. "Ready?"

She nodded and moved to the table, self-consciously aware of his gaze on her.

Dooley drank in her presence, loving the way she looked in the pink sundress, the floral scent that emanated from her. She was his Mary Ann tonight, her skin glowing with nothing artificial, her freckles endearingly present. He wanted her, not for a moment, not for a night, but for the rest of his life. Could he be enough for her? Could he get her to leave behind New York City and her dreams of being a star? He truly didn't know. But he did know he had to tell her he loved her. He couldn't keep his feelings for her trapped inside any longer. It was just a matter of picking the right moment.

They filled their plates, Dooley taking a heaping helping of the pasta and sauce, salad and bread sticks, Marina taking a bird's helping.

"You aren't eating very much," he observed.

"I'm not really that hungry, but everything looks delicious," she hurriedly added.

"I love pasta," Dooley said.

"You love food," she teased, beginning to relax as she realized he was going to keep the conversation light and easy.

"You're right." He laughed. "We ate a lot of pasta when I was growing up. Pasta, beans, potatoes, they're all cheap ways to feed a lot of people." He grinned.

"I'll bet you I know a hundred different ways to make a potato taste good."

"It must have been hard on your mother, trying to provide for all you kids," she observed thoughtfully.

Dooley nodded. "It was, but she never made us feel like burdens. She is a woman who loves to laugh. We may not have always been able to pay our bills, and there wasn't extra money for presents or fancy clothes, but our house was always filled with lots of laughter."

Marina smiled wistfully. "It must be nice, having such a big family."

"You should see us when we all get together on holidays. It's chaos, but a nice kind of chaos." Dooley took a bite of his bread stick, then continued. "My mother always stressed the importance of family. She said money got spent, fame was fleeting, but family was forever."

Marina felt dangerous wistful stirrings beginning inside her. She wondered how different she would be had she had that kind of a childhood, one filled with laughter, and family, and love. "Your mother sounds like a very smart woman."

Again he nodded. "Oh, she isn't book smart. She doesn't have much of a formal education. But she's heart smart." He grinned. "And I don't mean that she watches her cholesterol intake. I mean she trusts her instincts, listens to her heart." He looked at Marina thoughtfully. "She'd like you." More than that, Dooley knew his mother would look into Marina's eyes and see the need there, and Margaret James would turn herself inside out to try and help fill that need. She had a heart as big as a mountain.

"She sounds like somebody I would like, too," Marina said, focusing her attention on eating. Yes, she would probably like the woman who had raised a son like Dooley. She concentrated on her spaghetti. She didn't want to hear about Dooley's family. She didn't want to hear about how loving, how giving they were. They had nothing to do with her. They would never have anything to do with her.

"This sauce is magnificent," she said after taking a taste of the tangy, rich tomato sauce.

"It's an old family recipe," he answered.

"Do you serve this in your restaurants?"

He shook his head. "All my restaurants specialize in country cooking . . . the kind of cooking all mothers would do if they had the time and money."

"And you think a restaurant like that will be successful in New York?"

"All my marketing-research people tell me it will. They seem to think a Country Cookin' Restaurant will be a novelty here. Besides, the restaurants have already proved remarkably successful in other major cities."

"You've come a long way, haven't you?"

"Yes. There are times I'm sorry that I've moved away from the actual cooking end and instead find myself dealing more with the business of being a restaurateur. But for the most part, I'm happy with where my professional life is right now." He hesitated a moment then continued. "But more and more I'm aware that there are other things in life besides careers and business."

She looked down, refusing to meet his gaze, not wanting him to take this particular conversation any further.

"Marina . . . ?"

She looked up into his hypnotic green gaze and she tensed, knowing he was going to say something stupid, something that would make her crazy. She stiffened expectantly.

"I love you."

The words hung in the air for a moment, as if suspended by sheer force. A myriad emotions raced through Marina. For a moment she couldn't speak. His words had caused the air to whoosh out of her lungs.

"Dammit, Dooley, why did you have to go and say something like that?" Something inside of her snapped and she threw her napkin onto the table, needing to run, wanting to escape the vulnerability of his expression, the love shining from his emerald eyes.

She stood up and pushed her chair away, but before she could take a single step, his hand closed around her wrist.

"Please, Marina. Don't leave. I . . . I needed to say that. We need to talk about it. I don't think you're indifferent to me?" It was more a question than a statement.

"What difference does it make how I feel about you?" she asked, her voice quivering with emotion. Why did he have to say those words to her? It would have been so much easier to say goodbye if he hadn't told her he loved her.

"It makes all the difference in the world. If I know you love me, too, then I'm going to fight to make this relationship work."

He stood up and walked around the table to stand directly in front of her, not releasing his grip on her wrist. "Marina, I love you, and I want you to be a part of my life. I want you to marry me, be my wife."

Marina closed her eyes, wanting to be away from this man with his seductive Southern drawl, his eyes that promised so much. He stood so close to her she could feel the heat of his body, a welcome warmth that promised fires of passion, flames of desire.

"Marina, what we feel for each other, it doesn't come along every day. We've got something special. Can't you feel it?"

Yes, she felt it, but she steeled herself against the lure of him. She opened her eyes and looked at him sadly. "Dooley, this is crazy. It could never work. I belong here, and you belong back at Whispering Pines."

"I could change that," he replied, running a hand through his hair. "Hell, New York City isn't such a bad place. I could adjust."

Her love for him swelled up inside her, choking in her throat, bringing tears to her eyes as she realized the sacrifice he was willing to make for her. But she knew deep in her heart that wasn't an answer. "How long do you think you could be happy here?" she asked, her voice a mere whisper of truth. "How long would it be before you'd be miserable and homesick, and then you'd begin resenting me and my career, and before long the love would be dead and we'd be two shattered people trying to pick up the pieces."

"There's no way to know that's what would happen," he said, but his tone was hesitant. For a long moment they merely stood there, looking at each other.

"Are you so certain that acting can really make you happy?" he asked, his voice solemn, the light in his eyes dimmed somewhat.

She shrugged, somehow feeling defeated, like she had just lost an important fight. "I really don't know," she admitted. "But I know that I've worked all my life to get to the place where I am right now. I can't just throw it all away now. I have to see it through."

"And so you'll throw away what we feel for each other?" There was a hollowness in his voice that echoed in her heart.

She pulled her wrist from his grasp and stepped away. "I'm sorry," she whispered, her voice holding the pain of regret, of difficult choices, of heartbreak.

She headed for the door, but paused as he softly breathed her name. She turned and looked at him, seeing the way the candlelight painted him in red-gold tones. On cold, lonely nights it would be a memory that would haunt her with regret.

"A goodbye kiss...can't I at least have that?"

Before she could respond, he was there with his arms around her, pulling her tightly against him, breathing his love into her mouth. *A final memory,* she thought, losing herself in the fire of his lips. A final moment of madness that would torment her forever.

She allowed herself to get lost in his kiss. For every breath he gave her, she gave one back, until she no longer knew where he ended and she began. It was more than a meeting of two sets of lips, it was a yearning, a wish, a goodbye.

She tore her mouth from his and fumbled for the doorknob, thwarted by the tears that blurred her vision. She finally managed to yank open the door. "Goodbye, Dooley," she gasped, then she disappeared.

Chapter Ten

"Hey, Dooley? You home?" Gregory's voice drifted through the wood of Dooley's door.

Dooley stopped his packing and went to answer the door. "Come on in," he greeted the little man, motioning for him to have a seat on the sofa.

"What are you doing?" Gregory asked, noticing the open suitcase that lay on the floor. "You aren't leaving us, are you?"

"Not today. I'm catching a late flight Friday night," Dooley explained, folding the shirt he still held in his hands and placing it in the suitcase. "I just thought I'd start packing ahead of time."

Actually, he'd started packing to take his mind off Marina. Marina... funny how since the night she'd walked out of his apartment, he'd had no problem thinking of her as Marina instead of Mary Ann. She'd chosen to remain Marina and he could do nothing but accept her choice.

"Things didn't work out as you'd hoped?" Gregory sat down onto the sofa and looked at Dooley curiously.

"Sure they did, I found a terrific site for the new restaurant. I'm sure it's going to be a real winner."

"That's not what I'm talking about," Gregory returned with a note of censure. "I was talking about you and Marina."

With a sigh of frustration, Dooley sank down into the nearby chair. "No, things didn't go as I'd hoped."

"I was rooting for you, Dooley. I'd like to see Marina get out of this business while she still has her soul."

Dooley looked at him in surprise. "You don't think she can be happy being an actress?"

Gregory shrugged. "Who am I to say what will make her happy and what won't?" He hesitated a moment, then continued. "All I know is that Marina has a sort of frantic fervor where her acting is concerned. I think she's built up the experience in her mind and there's no way it can be all that she wants it to be. But of course, I could be wrong. Marina may be one who will make it in that crazy business."

Dooley sighed again and tugged at his beard thoughtfully. "I don't know how to fight this. If I was fighting another man, I could deal with that. But I'm fighting a dream, one that sustained her for a lot of years. I don't have any weapons to fight that kind of enemy."

"Love can be a pretty powerful weapon," Gregory observed.

Dooley looked at him helplessly. "But sometimes love isn't enough." Dooley fought down his feeling of despair. With every moment that ticked by and brought him closer to the plane flight that would take him home, his feeling of helplessness grew. "Is she good, Gregory?" Somehow that would make it easier for him to accept. "I mean, she's been in this city for over a year and has just now gotten her first real job. Is she good?"

"Yeah, she's pretty good. She just hasn't been lucky enough to get the breaks, at least until now. I wouldn't say she's the undiscovered Meryl Streep, but she does have talent. And you know you can't judge her talent by the amount of time it took her to get a job. Luck plays as important a part as talent in getting roles."

"So, what have you decided about a job?" Dooley asked, wanting to change the subject. It hurt too much to think about what might have been.

"I'd really like to talk to you more in depth about the manager job at the new restaurant." Gregory reached into his pocket and withdrew a sheet of paper. He unfolded it and handed it to Dooley. "This is my résumé. I'm afraid it's rather brief, but it does tell about the business courses I took a couple of years ago."

Dooley scanned it quickly. "You know the restaurant won't be ready to open for another three months. I won't need anyone before that time. If I decide to hire you, how will you survive until then?"

"I'll get by. I've still got some residuals coming in from a commercial I did a couple months ago."

"As far as I'm concerned, the job is yours."

"Hey, that's great," Gregory jumped up off the sofa and grasped Dooley's hand in an enthusiastic handshake. "I promise you won't be sorry. It will be the best-managed restaurant in all of Manhattan."

Dooley laughed at Gregory's enthusiasm. Dooley had always made all his business decisions on instinct, and that's what had prompted him to give Gregory the job. And his instincts were rarely wrong. He had a feeling Gregory would be an invaluable employee, loyal and true. Dooley also looked forward to having Gregory as a friend for a long time to come.

"I guess I'd better get out of here. I promised Josie we'd take the kids to a movie this afternoon." Gregory walked toward the door. "Funny, isn't it, about life? I mean, who would have thought three months ago that I would quit acting, get a job managing a restaurant and actually look forward to taking a couple of rug-rats to a movie about sewer dwellers?" Gregory shook his head ruefully. "I think life is the craziest role of all, don't you?"

"Gregory?" Dooley stopped him before he was all the way out the door. "What's the name of the theater where Marina is working?"

"The Trinity...why?"

"I thought I'd send her some flowers for opening night."

Gregory nodded with a sympathetic smile. "She'll like that." With a small wave, Gregory left.

The moment he was gone, Dooley also left his apartment. When he reached the street he signaled for a taxi.

"Trinity Theater," he told the driver, then settled back in the seat thoughtfully. Maybe she doesn't have the talent to match her ambition, he told himself, tugging on his beard. Perhaps Gregory was horribly prejudiced and Marina was really a terrible actress. After all, they were close friends. It wasn't out of the question to consider that Gregory would be less than objective. If she wasn't really talented, then Dooley wouldn't feel guilty about continuing his efforts to get her to marry him. If she was good...he refused to consider that possibility.

All too soon the driver pulled up before the theater. Dooley got out of the taxi slowly, like a condemned man going to his execution. There was only one chance for a call from the governor with a stay of execution, one thing that would save Dooley from a certain death, and that was if Marina was the most horrendous actress he'd ever seen. Only then would he feel it okay to pursue her with no holds barred.

The lobby of the theater was empty, so he went quietly through the double doors that were straight ahead. He found himself in the back of the darkened theater, the stage illuminated straight ahead. He slid into a seat in the back row.

"No, no, no!" A chubby, balding man jumped up from the front row and climbed up the stairs to the stage. "Ms. Walker, I've shown you three times…this is your mark, right here." He stomped his foot to emphasize the place where he wanted the actress to stand. "Now, let's try it again from the top of this scene." He paused to light the end of his stubby cigar, then went back to the front row.

Dooley watched all this with a sense of fascination, immediately becoming intrigued with the plot of the play. The leading lady was quite good, as was the male counterpart. The sets were not elaborate, but were adequate and other than occasional comments from the man in the front row, the play progressed smoothly.

Suddenly, she was onstage, her presence electrifying Dooley. She had only a few lines, but she delivered them perfectly and Dooley felt a chill of loss sweep over him. She had a presence that was undeniable, and her voice carried easily to him all the way in the back row. She was good, and Dooley knew there was no way he would bother her any longer. Maybe she had been right, this is where she belonged, thrilling audiences. He had no right to ask her to give up this for him.

He crept out of the theater, feeling as though a little piece of him had died.

* * *

Marina sat in front of her window, her apartment in darkness, her thoughts on the man across the way. She hadn't seen Dooley since the night she had run out of his apartment. But she felt his presence. Thoughts of him were like an open wound, still hurting with rawness. Eventually, she knew the pain would fade. It always did with time. It had taken her many years for the pain of her childhood to dim. She had a feeling it would take twice as long for thoughts of Dooley to no longer bring with them a soul-wrenching anguish.

Tomorrow night he would be gone. A silver plane would take him out of her life, wing him back to South Carolina and a place called Whispering Pines.

For the hundredth time, she wondered if she'd made the right choice in turning her back on Dooley and all that he offered.

She honestly didn't know if she'd made a mistake or not. All she did know was that she had to follow her head, not her heart. She'd set a course for herself long ago, and nothing and nobody could deter her, not even Dooley James and his personal brand of homespun loving.

She started to move away from the window, then hesitated, sensing his presence at his window. She could barely discern his silhouette, sturdy and solid, filling up the space. For a moment they remained silent, intensely aware of each other and the emotion that hung in the air between them.

"Dooley?" she finally called softly.

"I'm here, Marina," he answered in his sweet, Southern drawl.

For another long moment neither of them spoke. It was enough just to be there, window to window, connecting only with their thoughts. It was Marina who broke the silence once again. "So, you're leaving tomorrow night?"

"Yes . . . and your play opens tomorrow night."

Again there was a long silence, broken only by the intrusive sounds of the city at night.

So many things Marina wanted to say, so many emotions she needed to express, but what was the point? Why make the moment of farewell more difficult for both of them? Instead, she bit her lip, suppressing all that was contained within her.

Dooley waited for her to say something, needing to hear her say that she would miss him, that she was glad they'd met, anything. But the silence from her window was deafening. He fought the impulse to jump out of his window and into hers, ask her once more to reconsider. What was the point? She'd set her future trail, and it was one that led away from him.

"Well, I guess this is goodbye," he finally said softly.

"Yes, I guess it is," she returned.

"And not a moment too soon, if you ask me," the familiar gruff voice yelled from the window nearby.

Dooley smiled, realizing he was even going to miss the neighborhood grouch.

"Good night, Dooley," Marina whispered.

"Goodbye, Marina" was his reply.

Opening night. Marina stared at her reflection in the dressing-room mirror. This was the night she had waited for all her life. This was the night when her dreams began to come true.

"Damn, do you have any mascara? Mine's all dried up," Sandy Walker, the play's leading lady, asked Marina.

"Sure." Marina handed the older woman her tube of black mascara. "Are you nervous?" She looked at Sandy curiously, watching as the seasoned actress darkened her pale blond eyelashes.

"Nah. If this were a Broadway production with big bucks backing it, then maybe I'd work up a case of the jitters." She finished with her lashes and handed the tube back to Marina. "I figure we'll be lucky to get a four-week run out of this particular play."

"Four weeks of a play looks better on a résumé than nothing," Marina returned.

Sandy grinned at her. "You sound like me a couple of years ago. But you're right."

They were interrupted by a knock on the door. "Oh, is it time already?" Marina gasped, grabbing her stomach to still the butterflies fluttering within.

"Relax." Sandy laughed, checking her wristwatch. "We've still got at least thirty minutes before final call." She opened the dressing-room door to see an usher holding a bouquet of flowers.

"These are for Marina Burns," the young man explained, handing the flowers to Sandy.

"For you," Sandy said, closing the door and giving the bouquet to Marina.

Marina knew who they were from without looking at the card. Only Dooley would send the colorful profusion of wildflowers. No stiff and formal roses from the man from South Carolina. She set the bouquet on the dressing table and opened the card.

May all your dreams come true. Always, Dooley.

The butterflies began once again in her stomach as she looked at her wristwatch. In about four hours she would be on her way to the opening-night cast party and Dooley would be on his way to the airport.

She wasn't sure what exactly made her feel so sick, the thought of going out on the stage and performing or the thought of life without Dooley.

It's stage fright, she told herself, going back over to the grimy, warped mirror to complete her makeup. *This sick feeling in the pit of my stomach has nothing to do with Dooley.*

She shoved thoughts of Dooley out of her mind, concentrating on going over her lines in her head. *Focus,* she told herself. *Focus only on the play, on achieving your dreams.*

She turned as the door to the dressing room flew open and with a jangling of gold bracelets, Holiday Maxwell marched in, a handsome young man pausing just behind her.

"Marina, darling. I had to come back and see you before you went on." Holiday kissed her on the cheek, holding on to her face for a moment and staring deeply into Marina's eyes. "Are you ready?"

Marina nodded.

"Are you focused?"

"I think so," Marina replied.

Holiday patted her cheek and smiled wistfully. "Ah, Marina. You remind me of myself when I was your age. I had the same burning ambition, the same hunger inside. I see it all there in you." Holiday sighed. "It makes me remember the good days."

Marina smiled tremulously, finding it exciting that the legend of screen and stage saw herself in Marina.

"Well, we must find our seats." Holiday gave Marina's cheek a final pat, then with a jingle-jangle and a gesture to the handsome man, she swept out of the dressing room like a queen exiting a ball.

"Poor Holiday," Sandy said the minute the door was firmly closed.

Marina looked at her curiously. "Why do you say that?"

Sandy moved back in front of the mirror and began brushing her hair. "There's nothing more pathetic than an old actress with no stage."

"She doesn't seem too pathetic to me," Marina protested. "She teaches her drama classes, and she seems happy. And did you see that hunk who was with her?"

Sandy laughed and paused with the brush over her head. "Honey, that hunk is Craig Jeffries from an escort service. Holiday pays him to attend functions with her." Sandy shrugged and returned her attention to her hair. "But I guess that's the price some people pay to become legends."

Marina looked back at her own reflection, digesting what Sandy had just said. It seemed a dear price to pay for success, to end up alone. For the first time, Marina had an unpleasant vision of what happened to actresses when the applause died and the audience went home. This was part of the business she'd never considered before.

Before she'd had time to fully contemplate this new dimension, there was a knock on the door and a voice announced that the curtain was going up in two minutes. Sandy and Marina left the dressing room to take their places in the wings.

Suddenly, the play had begun. As Marina waited for her cue, she held her stomach, wondering how actresses did this every night of their lives. She felt sick, like she was going to throw up. She was terrified and couldn't control the trembling of her hands. Her legs felt like they might buckle beneath her. Yet it was a wonderfully exciting illness. The audience was there, responding to the people onstage. This was what it was all about. This was what she'd dreamed about since she was a child.

Then she was onstage, saying her lines, doing what she was supposed to do. The lights were bright on her face, like the warmth of a lover's touch. The scent of greasepaint was like the odor of success. She felt the audience reaching out to her, and she gave back.

It was over... at least for this night. Marina's part was done. She was exhausted, wrung out, the rush of moments before over like a barely remembered dream.

She stood in the wings, watching the rest of the play, finding herself distracted, continuously looking down at her wristwatch. In two hours Dooley would probably be calling for a taxi, getting ready to leave for the airport. The minutes ticked by, the play continued. Marina could hear the audience responding, laughing when they were supposed to, concentrating on the action on stage.

In one hour Dooley would be leaving for the airport, leaving to catch his plane back to South Carolina.

Finally, the play was over and they were all onstage, taking their final bows. Marina walked onstage to receive her applause. Again she felt the thrill of a rush as she returned to the stage. This was what it was all about... this is what she always wanted, to stand onstage and feel the audience's love. As she heard the audience clapping, she waited for the warmth of the crowd to fill her heart. She waited anxiously for the love she'd always thought she'd feel emanating from the people in the darkness in front of her.

There was nothing. Oh, sure, they clapped and it sounded nice. But it was a cold, impersonal sort of victory. They weren't cheering for her, they weren't clapping for Mary Ann Rayburn. They were cheering the performance of an actress. It had nothing to do with who she was.

She suddenly knew what happened to actresses when the applause died and the audience went home. They went back to their lonely homes... lonely because personal relationships were sacrificed, friendships were sacrificed. Is that what Marina wanted for herself? Was that the kind of life she'd always dreamed of?

I've made a mistake. The words reverberated inside her head, making her stomach convulse in shock. This wasn't what she wanted, this adulation of fickle strangers in the dark.

The minute the curtain came down for the final time, Marina raced into the dressing room and grabbed her purse. As she was running out the backstage door, Sandy spied her.

"Hey, Marina, aren't you coming to the cast party?"

"I can't. I've got something important to do," Marina replied, racing out the door and stopping at the curb where she frantically signaled for a taxi.

She gave the driver her address, then huddled in the back seat, trying to stop the trembling that had overtaken her. "Please...please don't let me be too late," she whispered. "Please let me get there before he leaves."

When the taxi pulled up at the curb in front of her apartment building, she threw the driver his money, then raced inside. She didn't bother waiting for the elevator, but instead hurried up the flights of stairs, her heart thudding painfully in her chest.

As she unlocked her door, she glanced at her watch. *Oh, God, please let me be in time to stop him.* She ran over to her window and leaned out. "Dooley?"

The apartment across the alleyway was dark. Tears burned at Marina's eyes when there was no answering reply. "Dooley, are you there?" *Please be there.* Still, no answer.

She squeezed her eyes tightly shut. Too late. Too late she had realized that Dooley held the key to making all her dreams come true. Too late she realized that Dooley and his love were all she needed to be happy.

"Marina...is that you?" His voice washed over her like a dream.

Her eyes flickered open in shock and she gasped her pleasure. "Oh, Dooley." Her voice caught on a sob. "I was afraid you'd gone."

There was a long moment of silence, then he answered, "Hell, Marina. I couldn't leave without you. I called three different taxis to take me to the airport, then called and canceled each one."

"Oh, Dooley." Marina stared across to his window, seeing his shadow there. "I love you, Dooley. I want you to take me to South Carolina."

"Hey, Dooley." The same old familiar voice filled the night from a window nearby. "Take her to South Carolina, take her to North Carolina, take her to Brooklyn... but *shut up!*"

Marina bit her lip to stifle a sudden giggle. She watched anxiously as Dooley stepped out of his window, onto the fire escape. He climbed down with the confidence of a man reaching out for an attainable dream. His footsteps were swift and sure on the rickety iron stairs. He hit the ground and began to climb up her fire escape, his face lit with a light that glowed more brightly than hundreds of spotlights. With her gaze on him, loving him, he climbed into her window and stood before her.

In seconds, she was in his arms, his lips speaking of love with hers. He tangled his hands in her hair and tugged gently, so she was looking up at him. "God knows, I tried to leave you. Then I got to thinking. Surely there's some way we can work out this problem between us. We could try Connecticut. I've heard it's nice there, and we'd be close enough for you to commute back here."

Marina shook her head. "I don't want Connecticut."

"If you want to be an actress, if the theater is important to you, then I'll build you one back home. I'll build you the biggest damn theater that little town has ever seen, and you can star in every production."

"I don't want a theater."

"Then tell me, what do you want?" His gaze burned into hers.

"I thought I wanted to be a star," she began. "I thought that's what I wanted. I believed that only the love and adulation of hundreds could fill the need in me. I truly believed that it would take the love of hordes of people to keep the loneliness away. But tonight I stood up on that stage and I listened to the applause, and I felt nothing." She looked up at him, loving the brilliant copper of his beard, the lines of his face... all the things that made him Dooley. "It was then I realized that the need I'd always felt had already been filled. I don't want to please a crowd, I don't want to please an audience. I just want to please the man I love."

Dooley looked into her eyes, his expression serious. "I went to one of your rehearsals. I saw you working, and you're good. Really good. I'm not sure it's fair for me to take you away from all that."

"You aren't taking me away from it." She smiled up at him with assurance. "I'm choosing to walk away from it. All I want to do is make my little mice for your restaurants, tell my stories to the kids who'll listen, and love you."

"Oh, Marina, I love you." His arms tightened around her.

"Dooley, my name is Mary Ann," she replied.

"I love you no matter what you want to call yourself," he replied. As his lips descended on hers again, Mary Ann heard the roar of the crowd, felt the warmth of love, experienced the feeling of being special, of mattering... it was all there in Dooley's heart. And it was more than enough for her.

Epilogue

"Happy?"

Mary Ann smiled up at Dooley, who looked splendid in a black tuxedo. They stood at the side of the hotel ballroom where their wedding reception was ongoing. "How could I be anything but happy?" she answered.

He put his arm around her and pulled her against him. She could feel the warmth of him through the white lace of her dress, but it was a heat that couldn't compete with that which shone from his eyes. "I thought we'd never see this day."

Mary Ann laughed. "Who would have thought the play would run nine weeks?"

"The longest nine weeks of my life," Dooley replied, then turned to greet a well-wisher. As he visited with the man whom Mary Ann remembered as one of his restaurant managers, she thought about the past three months.

From the moment she and Dooley had stood in her apartment and proclaimed their love for each other, Mary Ann had felt a peace within herself that she'd never known before. Gone was the frantic ambition, the hunger that drove her.

She'd enjoyed every minute of the play's run, but had no compulsion to pursue that career. She had a new life beginning, one ripe with promise, bursting with love.

"I always thought I'd lose my favorite baby-sitter when she became rich and famous. Who'd have thought I'd lose her to a good old country boy from South Carolina," Josie exclaimed as she moved next to Mary Ann.

"Who'd have thought," Mary Ann agreed with a laugh.

Josie gave her a quick hug. "I'm so happy for you, kid."

Mary Ann returned her hug. "What about you and Gregory? Is it possible we'll be hearing wedding bells soon for the two of you?"

Josie laughed and shrugged her shoulders. "You know Gregory. He's reluctant to leave his sexy bachelor status behind. But I'm working on changing his mind." Josie frowned suddenly, her gaze focused on the banquet table. "Oh, gotta go. I think I just saw Robert shovel a couple of canapés into his pocket."

As she hurried off, Mary Ann smiled. Gregory didn't have a chance. Over the last couple of months she'd watched Gregory and Josie's relationship develop and she had a feeling that before the end of the year, wedding bells would chime for the two of them.

She smiled at Dooley's mother approaching her. Dooley's entire family had flown in for the wedding. Even though Mary Ann had met Dooley's mom only briefly right before the ceremony, she'd immediately felt a warmth and kinship with her. How could she not love the woman who'd raised a man like Dooley?

The gray-haired woman took Mary Ann's hand in hers and smiled at her, her blue eyes radiating affection. "You've made my son very happy."

"No less than he's made me," Mary Ann returned.

"You know, I bought one of your little mice. They're wonderful, and they're selling like hotcakes."

Mary Ann nodded, pleasure sweeping through her. Yes, Dooley had told her the mice were a success. She'd been spending all of her spare time making more, indulging her creativity. The difference was that now the mice no longer reminded her of her lonely childhood. Dooley had banished the darkness of her past. "Did he tell you about his newest idea?"

Dooley's mother shook her head, and Mary Ann continued. "He thinks it would be nice if we planned a story hour in the restaurants once a week. While I'm telling stories, he can be in the kitchens, doing what he loves best."

"And what's that? Eating or cooking?"

"Probably both." Mary Ann laughed.

"Just what I like to see, the women in my life laughing together," Dooley said as he approached them.

"I think we're going to be doing a lot of that," his mother replied, once again smiling fondly at Mary Ann. She waved to somebody across the room and excused herself.

"She likes you," Dooley said the moment she'd left.

Mary Ann smiled. "And I like her."

Dooley put his arm around Mary Ann's waist and whispered into her ear. "When do you think we can make our escape from this party?"

She looked up into his eyes, seeing the warm green fires that beckoned her. "How about right now?"

Without further ado, Dooley and his new bride sneaked out the door, laughing as they ran for the elevator that would take them up to the honeymoon suite.

Alone in the elevator, he gathered her in his arms. "The moment I looked into your apartment and saw you, I think I knew then that you were the woman for me."

"And I was so certain that nothing could deter me from my career. But I hadn't counted on you, Dooley James. And I hadn't counted on love." She gasped, breathless as his lips touched hers in a kiss that held all the love of a lifetime, all the promise of forever.

*   *   *   *   *

HEARTLAND HOLIDAYS

**Christmas bells turn into wedding bells for the Gallagher
siblings in Stella Bagwell's *Heartland Holidays* trilogy.**

THEIR FIRST THANKSGIVING (#903) in November
Olivia Westcott had once rejected Sam Gallagher's proposal—
and in his stubborn pride, he'd refused to hear her reasons why.
Now Olivia is back...and it is about time Sam Gallagher listened!

THE BEST CHRISTMAS EVER (#909) in December
Soldier Nick Gallagher had come home to be the best man at his
brother's wedding—not to be a groom! But when he met single
mother Allison Lee, he knew he'd found his bride.

NEW YEAR'S BABY (#915) in January
Kathleen Gallagher had given up on love and marriage until she
came to the rescue of neighbor Ross Douglas...and the newborn
baby he'd found on his doorstep!

Come celebrate the holidays with Silhouette Romance!

HE'S MORE THAN
A MAN, HE'S
ONE OF OUR

EMMETT
Diana Palmer

What a way to start the new year! Not only is Diana Palmer's
EMMETT the first of our new series, FABULOUS FATHERS, but
it's her 10th LONG, TALL TEXANS and her 50th book for
Silhouette!

Emmett Deverell was at the end of his lasso. His three children
had become uncontrollable! The long, tall Texan knew they
needed a mother's influence, and the only female offering was
Melody Cartman. Emmett would rather be tied to a cactus than
deal with that prickly woman. But Melody proved to be softer
than he'd ever imagined....

Don't miss Diana Palmer's EMMETT, available in January.

Fall in love with our FABULOUS FATHERS—and join the
Silhouette Romance family!

Silhouette
R O M A N C E™

FF193

NORA ROBERTS

Love has a language all its own, and for centuries flowers have symbolized love's finest expression. Discover the language of flowers—and love—in this romantic collection of 48 favorite books by bestselling author Nora Roberts.

Two titles are available each month at your favorite retail outlet.

In December, look for:

Partners, **Volume #21**
Sullivan's Woman, **Volume #22**

In January, look for:

Summer Desserts, **Volume #23**
This Magic Moment, **Volume #24**

Collect all 48 titles and become fluent in

THE LANGUAGE of LOVE

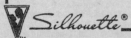

Silhouette®

OFFICIAL RULES • MILLION DOLLAR MATCH 3 SWEEPSTAKES
NO PURCHASE OR OBLIGATION NECESSARY TO ENTER

To enter, follow the directions published. **ALTERNATE MEANS OF ENTRY:** Hand print your name and address on a 3″ ×5″ card and mail to either: Silhouette "Match 3," 3010 Walden Ave., P.O. Box 1867, Buffalo, NY 14269-1867, or Silhouette "Match 3," P.O. Box 609, Fort Erie, Ontario L2A 5X3, and we will assign your Sweepstakes numbers. (Limit: one entry per envelope.) For eligibility, entries must be received no later than March 31, 1994. No responsibility is assumed for lost, late or misdirected entries.

Upon receipt of entry, Sweepstakes numbers will be assigned. To determine winners, Sweepstakes numbers will be compared against a list of randomly preselected prizewinning numbers. In the event all prizes are not claimed via the return of prizewinning numbers, random drawings will be held from among all other entries received to award unclaimed prizes.

Prizewinners will be determined no later than May 30, 1994. Selection of winning numbers and random drawings are under the supervision of D.L. Blair, Inc., an independent judging organization, whose decisions are final. One prize to a family or organization. No substitution will be made for any prize, except as offered. Taxes and duties on all prizes are the sole responsibility of winners. Winners will be notified by mail. Chances of winning are determined by the number of entries distributed and received.

Sweepstakes open to persons 18 years of age or older, except employees and immediate family members of Torstar Corporation, D.L. Blair, Inc., their affiliates, subsidiaries and all other agencies, entities and persons connected with the use, marketing or conduct of this Sweepstakes. All applicable laws and regulations apply. Sweepstakes offer void wherever prohibited by law. Any litigation within the province of Quebec respecting the conduct and awarding of a prize in this Sweepstakes must be submitted to the Régies des Loteries et Courses du Quebec. In order to win a prize, residents of Canada will be required to correctly answer a time-limited arithmetical skill-testing question. Values of all prizes are in U.S. currency.

Winners of major prizes will be obligated to sign and return an affidavit of eligibility and release of liability within 30 days of notification. In the event of non-compliance within this time period, prize may be awarded to an alternate winner. Any prize or prize notification returned as undeliverable will result in the awarding of that prize to an alternate winner. By acceptance of their prize, winners consent to use of their names, photographs or other likenesses for purposes of advertising, trade and promotion on behalf of Torstar Corporation without further compensation, unless prohibited by law.

This Sweepstakes is presented by Torstar Corporation, its subsidiaries and affiliates in conjunction with book, merchandise and/or product offerings. Prizes are as follows: Grand Prize—$1,000,000 (payable at $33,333.33 a year for 30 years). First through Sixth Prizes may be presented in different creative executions, each with the following approximate values: First Prize—$35,000; Second Prize—$10,000; 2 Third Prizes—$5,000 each; 5 Fourth Prizes—$1,000 each; 10 Fifth Prizes—$250 each; 1,000 Sixth Prizes—$100 each. Prizewinners will have the opportunity of selecting any prize offered for that level. A travel-prize option, if offered and selected by winner, must be completed within 12 months of selection and is subject to hotel and flight accommodations availability. Torstar Corporation may present this Sweepstakes utilizing names other than Million Dollar Sweepstakes. For a current list of all prize options offered within prize levels and all names the Sweepstakes may utilize, send a self-addressed, stamped envelope (WA residents need not affix return postage) to: Million Dollar Sweepstakes Prize Options/Names, P.O. Box 4710, Blair, [fj NE 68009.

The Extra Bonus Prize will be awarded in a random drawing to be conducted no later than May 30, 1994 from among all entries received. To qualify, entries must be received by March 31, 1994 and comply with published directions. No purchase necessary. For complete rules, send a self-addressed, stamped envelope (WA residents need not affix return postage) to: Extra Bonus Prize Rules, P.O. Box 4600, Blair, NE 68009.

For a list of prizewinners (available after July 31, 1994) send a separate, stamped, self-addressed envelope to: Million Dollar Sweepstakes Winners, P.O. Box 4728, Blair, NE 68009.   SWP-1292

VOWS
A series celebrating marriage
by Sherryl Woods

To Love, Honor and Cherish—these were the words that three generations of Halloran men promised their women they'd live by. But these vows made in love are each challenged by the tests of time....

In October—Jason Halloran meets his match in *Love #769*;
In November—Kevin Halloran rediscovers love—with his wife—in *Honor #775*;
In December—Brandon Halloran rekindles an old flame in *Cherish #781*.

These three stirring tales are coming down the aisle toward you—only from Silhouette Special Edition!

Experience the beauty of Yuletide romance with Silhouette Christmas Stories 1992—a collection of heartwarming stories by favorite Silhouette authors.

JONI'S MAGIC by Mary Lynn Baxter
HEARTS OF HOPE by Sondra Stanford
THE NIGHT SANTA CLAUS RETURNED by Marie Ferrarrella
BASKET OF LOVE by Jeanne Stephens

Also available this year are three popular early editions of Silhouette Christmas Stories—1986, 1987 and 1988. Look for these and you'll be well on your way to a complete collection of the best in holiday romance.

Plus, as an added bonus, you can receive a FREE keepsake Christmas ornament. Just collect four proofs of purchase from any November or December 1992 Harlequin or Silhouette series novels, or from any Harlequin or Silhouette Christmas collection, and receive a beautiful dated brass Christmas candle ornament.